I spent the first summer after the end of the war with distant relations in the country.

During those weeks, that village seemed to me an island of peace. One of the last places to have survived intact after the great storm that we had just weathered.

Years later, when life had gone back to normal and that summer was only a happy memory, I read about the same village in the paper.

My village had become the home of 'the murder farm', and I couldn't get the story out of my mind.

With mixed feelings, I went back.

The people I met there were very willing to tell me about the crime. To talk to a stranger who was nonetheless familiar with the place. Someone who wouldn't stay, would listen, and then go away again.

The Murder Farm

Andrea Maria Schenkel

Translated from the German by Anthea Bell

Quercus

First published in Great Britain in 2008 by Quercus
This paperback edition published in 2009 by

Quercus
21 Bloomsbury Square
London
WC1A 2NS

German original, *Tannöd*, first published by Edition Nautilus.

English translation Copyright © 2008 by Anthea Bell
Copyright © 2006 by Edition Nautilus

Published by agreement with Edition Nautilus.

The Litany for the Comfort of Poor Souls (for private use) printed
in the book is taken from *The Myrtle Wreath. A Spiritual Guide for Brides and
Book of Devotions for the Christian Woman*. Kevelaer 1922.

A CIP catalogue reference for this book is available
from the British Library

ISBN 978 1 84724 765 0

10 9 8 7 6 5 4 3 2 1

Typeset by Lindsay Nash
Printed and bound in Great Britain by Clays Ltd, St Ives plc.

Lord have mercy upon us!
Christ have mercy upon us!
Lord have mercy upon us!
Christ, hear us!
Christ, hear our prayer!
God the Father in Heaven, have mercy upon them!
God the Son, Redeemer of the world, have mercy upon them!
God the Holy Ghost, have mercy upon them!
Holy Trinity, Three in One, have mercy upon them!

Holy Virgin Mary, pray for them!
Holy Mother of God, pray for them!
Blessed Virgin of all virgins, pray for them!

Holy St Michael,
pray for them!
All holy angels and archangels,
All holy choirs of blessed spirits,
Holy St John the Baptist,
pray for them!

All holy patriarchs and prophets,
Holy St Peter,
Holy St Paul,
Holy St John,
pray for them!

All holy apostles and evangelists,
Holy St Stephen,
Holy St Lawrence,
pray for them!

All holy martyrs,
Holy St Gregory,
Holy St Ambrose,
pray for them!

Holy St Jerome,
Holy St Augustine,
pray for them!

All ye holy bishops and confessors,
All ye holy Fathers of the Church,
All ye holy priests and Levites,
All ye holy monks and hermits,
pray for them!

He enters the place early in the morning, before day-break. He heats the big stove in the kitchen with the wood he has brought in from outside, fills the steamer with potatoes and water, puts the steamer full of potatoes on the stove-plate.

He goes out of the kitchen, down the long, windowless corridor and over to the cowshed. The cows have to be fed and milked twice a day. They stand side by side in a row.

He speaks to them quietly. He is in the habit of talking to animals while he works in the shed with them. The sound of his voice seems to have a soothing effect on the cattle. Their uneasiness appears to be lulled by the regular sing-song of that voice, the repetition of the same words. The calm, monotonous sound relaxes them. He's known this kind of work all his life. He enjoys it.

He spreads a layer of fresh straw over the old one, fetching it from the barn next door. There is a pleasant, familiar smell in the shed. Cows don't smell like pigs. There's nothing sharp or assertive about their odour.

After that he fetches hay. He gets that from the barn too.

He leaves the connecting door between the barn and the cowshed open.

While the animals feed, he milks them. He is a little worried about that. The cows aren't used to being milked by him. But his fears that one of them will refuse to let him milk her had been unfounded.

The smell of the cooked potatoes drifts over to the cowshed. Time to feed the pigs. He tips the potatoes out of the steamer and straight into a bucket, where he crushes them before taking them to the pigs in their sty.

The pigs squeal when he opens the pigsty door. He tips the contents of the bucket into the trough and adds some water.

That's his work done. Before leaving the house he makes sure the fire in the stove is out again. He leaves the door between the barn and the cowshed open. He pours the milk from the cans straight on the dunghill. Then he puts the cans back in their place.

He would go back to the cowshed that evening. He'd feed the dog, who always cringes away into a corner, whimpering, when he arrives. He'd tend the animals. And while he worked he would always take great care to give a wide berth to the heap of straw in the far left-hand corner of the barn.

Betty, aged 8

Marianne and me always sit together in school. She's my best friend. That's why we always sit with each other.

Marianne specially likes my mama's yeast dumplings. When my mama bakes those dumplings I always take one to school for Marianne, or to church if it's a Sunday. I took her one that Sunday, but then I had to eat it myself because she wasn't at church.

What do we do together? Well, we play games, like cops and robbers, catch, hide and seek. In summer we sometimes play shops at my house. We make ourselves a little stall by the kitchen garden fence. Mama always lets me have a table-cloth and we can put things out on it: apples, nuts, flowers, coloured paper, anything we can find.

Once we even had chewing-gum, my auntie brought it. It tastes lovely, like cinnamon. My auntie says the children in America eat it all the time. My auntie works for the Yanks, you see. And now and then she brings us chewing-gum and chocolate and peanut butter. Or bread in funny green cans. Once last summer there was even ice-cream.

My mama doesn't like that so much, because Auntie Lisbeth's boyfriend comes from America too and he's all black.

Marianne's always saying her papa is in America as well, and he's going to come and fetch her very soon, she's sure he is. But I don't believe it. Because Marianne does tell fibs sometimes. Mama says you shouldn't tell fibs, and when Marianne tells another of her stories we quarrel. Then we usually each take our things away from the shop and we can't go on playing and Marianne goes home.

The Christ Child brought me a dolly for Christmas, and Marianne was very envious. She only has a really old one, it's a wooden dolly and it used to be her mama's. So then Marianne started telling stories again. How her papa is coming soon to take her away to America. I told her I wouldn't go on being her friend if she kept telling so many fibs. After that she didn't say any more about it.

Sometimes we go tobogganing in the meadow

behind our farm. There's a hill which is great for tobogganing, everyone in the village always goes there. If you don't brake in time you shoot right down into the hedge. Then there's usually trouble at home. Marianne has to bring her little brother along sometimes, when she's looking after him. He clings to your skirts all the time. I don't have any little brother, just a big sister, but that's not always much fun either. She often makes me really mad.

When Marianne's little brother fell over in the snow he started crying and he'd wet his pants too, and then Marianne had to go home and there was bad trouble. Because she hadn't looked after him properly and he'd wet his pants again and so on. Then she was very sad in school next day and told me she wanted to go away because her grandpa is so strict and so is her mama.

A few days ago she told me the magician was back. She'd seen him in the woods, she said, and she knows he'll take her to her papa. Yes, she said, she saw the magician. She told me that story once before, last autumn, right after school began and I didn't believe her, there's no such thing as magicians, and you bet your life there's no such thing as magicians who can magic you a papa who's supposed to be in America. So then I quarrelled with her again and she cried and said there is so a magician, and he has all coloured bottles in his rucksack and other coloured things and sometimes he just sits there humming to himself. So he must be a magician, just like in our reading book at school. Then I shouted, 'Liar, liar, pants on fire!' and she cried and ran home. And because she wasn't in school on Saturday and she loves my mama's yeast dumplings so much, I took one to church for her on Sunday. But she wasn't there either. Mama said because none of them were there maybe they'd gone to visit family. Over in Einhausen where her grandpa's brother lives. So I just ate the dumpling myself.

Marianne lies in bed awake. She can't get to sleep. She hears the wind howling. It sweeps over the farm like the Wild Hunt. Grandma's often told her stories about the Wild Hunt and the Trud, an evil spirit in female form. She always tells them on the long, dark, frosty nights between Christmas and New Year.

'The Wild Hunt races on before the wind, fast as the storm-clouds or even faster. The huntsmen are mounted on horses as black as the Devil,' Grandma had told her. 'Wrapped in black cloaks. Hoods drawn right down over their faces. Eyes glowing red, they race on. If anyone's rash enough to go out and about on such a night, the Wild Hunt will pick him up. At the gallop,' said Grandma. 'Just like that – got 'im!'

And she made a snatching movement with her hand, as if seizing something to extinguish it.

'Got 'im! And they take the poor fellow high up in the air and sweep him away with them. Up, up and away to the clouds, they sweep him right up into the sky. He has to go with the stormy wind. The hunt never lets him go again, the hunt howls and laughs with scorn. Ho, ho, ho', laughed Grandma in a deep voice.

Marianne could almost see the Wild Hunt picking a man up and laughing as it carried him away.

'And what happens then, Grandma?' Marianne asked. 'Doesn't he ever come down again?'

'Oh yes, oh yes', replied Grandma. 'Sometimes he comes down again, sometimes not. The Wild Hunt drags the poor devil on with it as long as it likes. Sometimes it puts him down again quite gently once it's had its fun. Sometimes. But mostly the poor man's found somewhere next morning with all his bones broken. His whole body all scratched and bruised, smashed to pieces. Many a man's never been seen again. The Wild Hunt has taken him straight to the Devil.'

Marianne keeps thinking about the story of the Wild Hunt. She'd never leave the house in a storm like this. The Wild Hunt isn't going to get her. Not likely!

She lies awake for a long time. How long she doesn't know. Her little brother sleeps in the same room. The beds are arranged so that they lie almost side by side. She in her bed, he in his small cot.

She hears his calm, regular breathing, they're lying so close. He breathes in and out. Sometimes, when she can't sleep, she listens to that sound in the night, tries to match her own breathing to his, breathes in when he breathes in, breathes out when he breathes out.

That sometimes helps, and then she gets tired too and falls asleep herself. But it doesn't work tonight. She's lying there awake.

Should she leave her bed? Grandpa will be terribly cross again. He doesn't like it when she gets up in the night and calls for her mother or her grandmother.

'You're old enough to sleep alone now', he says, and sends her back to bed.

There's a line of light shining under the door. Only faintly, but she sees a narrow strip of light.

So there's still somebody awake. Her mother, maybe? Or Grandma?

Marianne plucks up all her courage and puts her bare feet out of bed. It's cold in the room. She pushes the covers aside. Very quietly, so as not to wake her little brother, she tiptoes to the door. Cautiously, in case the floorboards creak.

Slowly, carefully, she pushes the door handle down and quietly opens the door. She steals down the passage and into the kitchen.

There's still a light on in the kitchen. She sits at the window and looks out into the night. It gives her the creeps, and she starts shivering in her thin nightie.

Then she notices that the door to the next room is ajar.

Her mother must have gone to the cowshed, Marianne

thinks. She opens the door to the next room wide. Another door opens out of that room into the passage leading to the cowshed and the barn.

She calls for her mother. For her grandmother. But there is no answer.

The little girl goes down a long, dark feed alley. She hesitates, stops. Calls for her mother again, for her grandmother. Rather louder this time. Still no answer.

She sees the cattle in the shed chained to the iron rings of the feeding trough. The cows' bodies move calmly. The place is lit only by an oil lamp.

Marianne sees the door to the barn standing open at the end of the feed alley.

Her mother will be in the barn. She calls for her mother again. There's still no answer.

She goes on along the feed alley towards the barn. She stops again at the door, undecided. She can't hear a single sound in the darkness. She takes a deep breath and goes in.

Holy St Mary Magdalene,
pray for them!
Holy St Catherine,
pray for them!
Holy St Barbara,
pray for them!

All ye blessed virgins and widows,
pray for them!
All ye saints of God,
pray for them!

Be merciful unto them! Spare them, O Lord!
Be merciful unto them! Deliver them, O Lord!

Babette Kirchmeier,
civil servant's widow, aged 86

Marie, ah yes, Marie.

She was my household help, yes. Well, until I went into the old folks' home.

That's right, my household help, Marie was. She was a good girl. A real good girl. Always did everything so neat and nice. Not like the young things now, gadding about the whole time, flirting with boys.

No, Marie wasn't like that. A good girl, Marie was.

Not all that pretty, but good and hard-working. She kept the whole place going for me.

I'm not so good on my legs any more, you see, that's why I'm in the home.

I don't have any children, and my husband died nearly fifteen years ago. It'll be fifteen years in June, on the twenty-fourth.

Ottmar, now, he was a good man. A good man.

So Marie came to help me in the house because my

legs didn't work so well any more. Ah, my legs, it's a long time since they worked well. When you get old there's a lot doesn't work as well as it used to, not just your legs. Growing old is no fun, you take my word for it, that's what my mother always said. No, it's no fun.

Once upon a time I could run like the wind. I was always going dancing with my Ottmar, God rest his soul. To the tea dance in the Odeon on Sunday afternoons. That was back before the war. Ottmar was a good dancer. We got to know each other at a dance, still in the Kaiser's time, that was. Oh, he was a dashing fellow, my Ottmar in his uniform. Ottmar was in the army then, he's been dead nearly fifteen years now.

Time passes by, time passes by. I had that trouble with my hip. We're none of us getting any younger, are we?

That's when Marie came to help me in the house. She slept in the little bedroom. She didn't ask for much, not Marie. A bed, a chair, a table and a cupboard, that's all she needed.

So in January, let me think now, yes, it was January when I went into the old folks' home, because I don't walk so well these days. Not so well at all. Yes, that's when Marie went to her sister's.

I didn't know she has a job as a maid now. But that would just suit Marie. A good hard worker. Didn't talk much. That suited me fine, because I can't be doing with those talkative young things. Chatter, chatter, chatter all day long, while the house goes to rack and ruin.

Yes, Marie was my household help, that's right. Well, until I went into the old folks' home. It was January I went into the old folks' home. A good honest household help, Marie was. A real good girl. Ever so good, she was. Always did everything so neat and nice.

I think I'm getting tired. I fancy a nap now. A person needs a lot of sleep when she gets old, you know. Many old folk can't sleep, but me, I need a lot of sleep. I always did like my sleep.

Oh, now what was it you were asking me? I've quite forgotten, dear me, it's old age, you know. You were asking me about Marie. Yes, yes, Marie. She was a good girl, Marie was, willing and hard-working.

What's she doing these days?

Isn't she at her sister's?

Oh, I'm so tired, I really fancy a nap now. You know, when a person gets old she needs her sleep.

Winter refuses to give way to spring this year. It is much colder than usual this season. There's been alternate rain and snow since early March. The grey of the morning mists lingers all day.

At last, on Friday morning, it clears slightly. The dark, grey-black clouds lift a little. Now and then the cloud cover breaks entirely, and the first rays of the spring sun shine tentatively through.

At midday, however, the sky grows dark again, and in the afternoon rain begins falling once more. It is so gloomy that you might think the day was already coming to an end, and night was falling.

Two figures, clad entirely in black, are on the move in this dim light. They are making for the only farm anywhere near. One of them is pushing a bicycle, the other carries a rucksack. The farmer, who has just left the house to go to the sheds and stables, prudently lets his dog off its leash. Only when the two figures have almost reached the farm does he see that they are both women.

He whistles the dog back and holds it firmly by the collar.

One of the two women, the one with the rucksack on her back, asks the way. They're looking for the Danner family's farm in Tannöd, she says. They've lost their way in the poor light. Can he help them? Does he know how to get to the farm?

'Over there, beyond the last field, turn left into the woods and you can't miss it,' he replies.

The two of them go on. The man puts his dog on its chain again and thinks no more about the couple.

Traudl Krieger,
sister of Marie the maid, aged 36

Early in the morning that Friday, I helped our Marie pack all her belongings. She didn't have much, enough to fill a rucksack and a bag too, that's all. No, it really wasn't much.

I'd promised to go with her when she started her new job. She didn't want to go out there alone, because she didn't know the way. So I gave her my promise. Gave her my promise...

It was fine first thing in the morning. But it was midday before we started off at last. The weather was nothing special by then. My mother-in-law came to look after the kids while I was gone.

My husband Erwin was still at work. He has to be on the building site early, he's a brickie. Never comes home until late on a Friday. Not that he has to work such long hours, no. But he gets his wages on Friday, and then he goes to the pub after work.

Usually he comes home late and drunk. That's men for you; drinking in the pub they forget everything, wife, children, just about everything.

When we set off, Marie and me, it hadn't begun raining yet. The weather was still reasonable. A lot of dark clouds in the sky, but on the whole the weather wasn't that bad. We'd had nothing but rain and snow over the last few weeks.

I carried the rucksack, and our Marie strapped her bag on the carrier of the bike. Now and then I helped her to push it.

I'd borrowed the bike and the rucksack from my neighbour the miller's wife. Erwin takes our own bike to work with him, and I didn't want to walk the whole way back. I thought I'd get home quicker on a bike.

Frau Meier who keeps the shop, she told me just how to get there. She told me about the vacant position in the first place.

'Your sister Marie's a good strong young woman. She can turn her hand to anything, and she's not work-shy. Over at the Danner farm their maid's walked out. They're looking for a new one. Just the thing for your Marie.' That's what she said.

Frau Meier in the shop always knows everything. People come from all around here to see her when a new maid's wanted, or a farm-hand, and they tell her all the news too, who's died, who's had a baby. Even if you're looking for someone to marry you just have to go to her. She can get the right couple together. Then her husband is the go-between and fixes up the wedding.

Marie had been with us in our little place since January. She's not demanding, well, you can't be, not with us.

Our place has two bedrooms, one for the children and one for us. It has a kitchen that's our living-room too and its own WC, not one for the whole floor of a building where you have to stand in line and wait for the others to be finished.

The place is big enough for Erwin, our three children and me, but with Marie as well space was very tight.

Marie was sleeping on the sofa in the kitchen living-room. It wasn't going to be for ever, really not, just for the time being. That's why I was so pleased about the job.

And after she came to us, our Marie was with my brother for three weeks. In February, that was. My brother has a little farm, just a smallholding. Our parents left it to him. My brother's wife wasn't well, so our Marie went to help out.

Marie was a good girl, you see. A really good girl. She could work hard, oh yes, she could, and she liked to work, but she was a simple soul too.

I mean, she was a little bit backward. Not mentally handicapped or that, just a bit kind of simple, and she was good-natured.

When our sister-in-law was better Marie came back to us. Marie never got on too well with our brother. He was always going on at her, she couldn't do anything right, not for him. He's been a grouch all his life, he won't ever change.

I'm younger than Marie, that's true, eight years younger, but to me our Marie was always the little sister I had to look after. When our mother died I mothered Marie instead of her. Our father died a long time ago too, he died just after Mother. Consumption, that's what the doctor said.

It'd be easy for anyone to take advantage of our Marie that wanted to. She always did as she was told, she never asked questions. Like Mother always said, the easy-going are usually good at heart too.

Well, Marie wasn't so much easy-going, but she was far too good at heart. She'd have worked for no wages, just for board and lodging. That was our Marie. Poor creature.

Up till New Year, our Marie had a job with Frau Kirchmeier. Babette Kirchmeier. Frau Kirchmeier was a widow, and Marie kept house for her as best she could. But Frau Kirchmeier had been going downhill fast. In the end she could hardly walk, and she was getting a bit confused. So then she went into the old folks' home, she's got no children who could have taken her in, poor Frau Kirchmeier. So our Marie lost her job.

And like I said, I'd promised Marie to go to the Danner farm with her.

From what Frau Meier told me, it should have taken us an hour and a half to get there, but the weather was getting worse and worse.

It turned really dark, and a squally wind was blowing. I keep on thinking we never ought to have gone, not in that weather. Then everything would be different now.

Well, we left our place around two, and by three-thirty or so we were hopelessly lost. So we wandered around for a while. Then we went back again a little way to the last farm we'd passed.

When we got there we asked our way.

Last field on the left, take the path through the woods, you can't miss it, the man said.

And it started raining again in the woods, so when we finally reached the farm we were sopping wet. It's a very isolated place, you know. I'd never have thought it was so far out in the country. If I'd known I'd never have let our Marie go there. Never. Out there in Tannöd, there was only the old lady at home, she opened the door to us. I didn't see anyone else. Only the old lady and the little boy.

A pretty child, two years old, I'd say, with lovely golden curls.

Marie took to the child on sight, I could see that, our Marie likes kids. But the old lady was very odd, she looked at us so suspiciously. Hardly passed the time of day. We hung our wet jackets over a chair. Close to the stove to dry. Old Frau Danner never said a word all the time. I tried to get her talking. I mean, there's questions to be asked when someone new comes to a farm. But no, we couldn't get anywhere with her, though the little boy was already clinging to Marie's skirt after five minutes and laughing.

And our Marie was laughing with him.

The kitchen was just like the farmyard, old and gloomy, and a little bit grubby too. The old lady was wearing an apron that could have done with a good wash. And the little boy's face was dirty.

I sat there with my sister Marie on the bench by the tiled stove for an hour, and in all that time old Frau Danner said maybe five sentences. Strange, surly folk, I said to myself.

At the end of an hour I put on my jacket, didn't want to go home in the dark. The jacket was nearly dry by this time and I wanted to set off straight away.

'I'll have to go home now, it's getting dark. I don't want to lose my way again,' I told Marie.

Then I met old Frau Danner's daughter on the doorstep.

Right there in the doorway.

We had a word or so, she was a bit friendlier than the old lady, and then I went out of the door. Our Marie came with me. I pushed the bike through the garden gate and said goodbye to her at the fence. She didn't look all that happy, I think she'd rather have gone back home with me. I could see how she felt, but what could I do? There was nothing else for it.

It almost broke my heart. I just wanted to get away from there quick. I told our Marie, 'I hope you like it. If not we'll find you something else.'

Marie only said, 'Oh, I'll be fine.'

I ought to have just taken her away with me. Something else would have come up. I'm certain it would. But I turned away and rode off on the bike. When our Marie called to me again I stopped and got off the bike.

Our Marie ran after me and gave me a big hug. Squeezed me tight. As if she never wanted to let go. I really had to tear myself away and get on the bike in a hurry.

I pedalled away like mad. I didn't want to stop again.

The house, the farm, no, I wouldn't even want to be buried there, I said to myself. It shook me, that place did.

How can anyone stand it out there with those people? Poor Marie, how would she be able to stand it? I was so upset, my chest felt tight, but what else was I to do? Marie couldn't sleep on our sofa any more, and Erwin was tired of it all too, he'd wanted to be rid of her long ago. I pedalled and pedalled. I didn't stop. I just wanted to get away, right away!

I wanted to get away from my guilty conscience as well.

After a while there was water running down my cheeks. I thought at first it was because the cycling made me sweat so much. But then I realized it was tears.

Marie goes to her room next to the kitchen straight after supper.

It is a small room. A bed, a table, a chest of drawers and a chair, there's no space for anything else.

The wash-basin and jug stand on the chest of drawers.

A small window opposite the door. If she goes to the window, which way will she be looking? Maybe towards the woods? She'll know in the morning. Marie would like to see the woods from her window.

The window sill is covered with dust. So is the table, so is the chest of drawers. The room has been standing empty for some time. The air is stale and musty. Marie doesn't mind.

She opens the drawer in the table. There's an old newspaper cutting inside, yellow with age. And a pillowcase button and the metal screw-top of a preserving jar. Marie closes the drawer again.

The bed stands to her right. A simple brown wooden bedstead. The quilt has a blue and white cover, and so does the pillow.

Sighing, Marie sits down on her bed. She stays there for a while, looking around her room.

Giving her thoughts free rein.

She misses Traudl and the children. But it's nicer sleeping in a bed than on the sofa, and she won't have to see Erwin for a while now either.

Erwin didn't like her, Marie sensed that as soon as she moved to Traudl's place at New Year. It was the way he came through the door, no greeting, no handshake, nothing. He just asked Traudl, 'What's she doing here, then?' And he jerked his head Marie's way without even looking at her.

'She'll be staying with us until she finds a new job.' That was all Traudl said.

'I don't like other folk living off of me,' was all he said in return.

She, Marie, acted as if she hadn't heard him say that. But it hurt, because Erwin is such an oaf. She's never told her sister so, but she's thought it all the same.

He thought she was 'stupid', and 'simple', 'mental', 'not quite right in the head', she's heard him say all those things and more too, but she's never protested. Because of Traudl and because of the children.

Thank God there are children here on this farm too, thinks Marie.

She gets on well with children. She once found a motto on a page in a calendar saying, 'Children are the salt of the earth'. She took note of that. She likes those old calendar mottos, and when she meets a specially nice child she takes out the page from the calendar and reads the old saying over and over again.

Marie sighs, gets off the bed, starts putting her things away in the chest of drawers. Begins settling into her room. She stops again and again. Sits down on her bed. Her arms keep dropping to her lap, limp, heavy as lead. She keeps thinking back to the past. Thinks of Frau Kirchmeier and how much she liked working for the old lady. Even if she was getting more and more peculiar.

Thinks of her brother Ott. He was the same sort as Erwin. You had to watch out with him. She'd been helping at his home a few weeks back when his wife was so poorly. She was glad to get away again.

She pulls herself together. No use sitting around all the time thinking about life, Marie tells herself. She must finish settling in and go to sleep, so that she can get up early in the morning. She's wasted enough time already.

She carefully goes on putting her possessions away. Keeps daydreaming, her thoughts stray all the time, she thinks of that first meal with her new employers.

The farmer, a big, strong man, silent. Didn't say much all through supper. He just gave her a brief good evening when he came in. A firm handshake, a glance sizing her up, that was all.

His wife, very silent too. Older than her husband. Careworn, tight-lipped. It was the wife said grace.

The daughter, now, she was nice to Marie. Asked if she had other brothers and sisters besides Traudl, asked about any nieces and nephews, what their names were and how old.

I could get on all right with her, thinks Marie.

And then the children...

The children in this house were nice. Nice kids, specially the little boy. He smiled at her straight away. He kept wanting to play. She joked with him. Took him on her knee and played 'Ride a cock-horse', the way she always did with her sister's children. Let him slide off her lap with a bump. The little boy had gurgled with laughter.

When their mother sent the children to bed Marie rose to her feet too.

'I'll go to my room now,' she said, 'I have to put my things away. Then I can start work first thing in the morning.'

She wished them all good night and went to her room.

But she's planning to stay at this farm only until she finds something better, she knows that now. Although the children are nice, and the farmer's daughter is someone she could get on with. The farm is too far out in the country, she'd like to be closer to Traudl.

Marie has almost finished tidying her things away. Just the rucksack to unpack now.

Outside, the weather is even worse. The wind is blowing harder and harder, a stormy wind.

I hope our Traudl got home all right, she thinks.

The window doesn't fit particularly well, the wind blows through the cracks in the frame. Marie feels a draught. She turns to the door. It is standing slightly ajar, and Marie goes to close it. Then she sees the door slowly opening wider and wider, creaking. She stares with incredulous amazement at the widening gap.

Marie can't make up her mind what to do. She just stands there, rooted to the spot. Eyes turned towards the door. Until she is felled to the ground without a word, without a sound, by the sheer force of the blow.

From all evil,
deliver them, O Lord!
From Thy anger,
deliver them, O Lord!
From the rigour of Thy justice,
deliver them, O Lord!
From the gnawing worm of conscience,
deliver them, O Lord!
From their long and deep affliction,
deliver them, O Lord!
From the torments of the purifying fire,
deliver them, O Lord!
From the terrible darkness,
deliver them, O Lord!
From the dreadful weeping and wailing,
deliver them, O Lord!
By Thy miraculous conception,
deliver them, O Lord!
By Thy birth,
deliver them, O Lord!
By Thy sweet name,
deliver them, O Lord!
By Thy baptism and Thy holy fasting,
deliver them, O Lord!
By Thy boundless humility,
deliver them, O Lord!

In the morning he usually gets up before dawn.

Slips on his trousers and goes down the corridor to the kitchen.

Once there, he gets the fire in the stove going with a few logs of wood.

Fills the little blue enamel pan and puts it on the stove.

Washes his face quickly with cold water from the kitchen tap.

Waits a few minutes for the water in the pan to come to the boil.

The can of chicory coffee stands on the shelf above the stove. He moves the pan of simmering water to one side and adds two spoonfuls of ground coffee. He turns, takes his cup from the kitchen dresser on the opposite wall, gets the tea-strainer out of the drawer. He pours the coffee into the cup through the strainer. Crumbles a slice of bread into the liquid to make a mush. He sits down at the table in the corner of the room with his cup, spoons the soaked bread out of the coffee. Sitting in front of the window, with the door behind him, he looks out into the darkness.

In summer he likes to sit on the bench behind his house and drink his coffee there. He listens to the birds' dawn chorus in the air that is still cool and pure. Bird after bird strikes up its song. Always in the same order, never changing. From where he sits he can hear them singing while the sun rises above the horizon.

He empties his cup and puts it down in the kitchen. The farm is awake now, and he goes about his day's work. Usually in silence at this early hour. Alone with himself and his thoughts. By the time day is clearly distinct from night, those precious moments of leisure are long past.

That's in summer.

In winter, he sits at the kitchen window where he is sitting now, looking out, impatient for the days to lengthen soon, so that he can enjoy his daily morning ritual again.

Hermann Müllner,
teacher, aged 35

I don't know that I can help you much, because I
didn't arrive here until the start of this school
year. I was appointed to this school in early
September. And there's been so much to do, I
haven't yet had time to get to know the country
people out here better.

I teach the Year Two children all subjects
except Religious Instruction. Our parish priest
Father Meissner teaches them that.

Little Maria-Anna, that was her real name, was
in my class.

She was a quiet pupil, very quiet. Rather
reluctant to speak up in lessons. Seemed a little
dreamy. Not particularly good at spelling, stumbled over the words slightly when she read
aloud. Arithmetic, yes, she was rather better at
arithmetic. Otherwise nothing much about her
struck me.

Her best friend, as far as I know, was Betty.

Betty sat beside her. Now and then the girls whispered to each other in lessons, the way girls do with their friends. Girls always have a great deal to talk about, so their attention sometimes wanders.

But when I told them not to do it, they were quiet at once.

I noticed little Maria-Anna's absence at once on the Saturday. That's why I asked the rest of the class whether anyone knew where the child was. Unfortunately no one did. When she still didn't turn up for lessons on Monday, I made a note of it in the class register.

It was just the same as other school days. We said morning prayers at the beginning of lessons, as we do every day, and as always we remembered in our prayers those pupils who were absent because of illness.

That's perfectly normal, we always do it, it's nothing out of the ordinary. After all, at that point I still had no idea how important our prayers for little Maria-Anna were.

Sometimes pupils don't turn up for school, but usually their parents write an excuse note afterwards, or if the child has a brother or sister at the school then the note comes on the first day a boy or girl is absent, explaining why.

So I decided that if there was still no excuse note for the girl on Tuesday I'd cycle out to Tannöd and her grandparents' farm. I was planning to go as soon as school was over that Tuesday, but then something happened to keep me here. Ever since I've been wondering whether maybe I ought to have cycled out earlier. But would that have helped little Maria-Anna? I don't know.

Ludwig Eibl,
postman, aged 32

The Danner family's farm is almost at the end of my round. I've been doing the same round these last six months. I pass the place almost every day. Well, certainly three times a week. Because old Danner takes the local newspaper, and that comes out three times a week. On Monday, on Wednesday and on Friday.

If there's no one in I'm supposed just to leave their post by the window next to the front door, that's what old Danner agreed with me.

So I was out there on the Monday, and when no one came to the door I left the post where we'd agreed. I looked in through the window too, but there wasn't anyone around.

It happens now and then. I mean, it happens there's no one at home. No, it's not unusual. That time of year, folk are often out chopping wood. Everyone's needed then, nobody stays on the farm.

The dog, yes, could be it barked. Yes, I'm sure it barked. But that's all I can remember. I mean, dogs always bark when I arrive. I don't listen any more. All part of a postman's job.

When I got back on my bike I did turn round once, checking that my bag was balanced on the carrier properly. When it's getting empty it easily slips. So when I looked round, yes, I saw the house again.

Was there any smoke coming out of the chimney? What questions you do ask! I've no idea if there was smoke coming out of the chimney. Didn't notice anything.

Took no notice of any of it anyway.

You want me to be honest, I didn't much like them at that farm. Old Danner was a suspicious sod. A loner. His wife Frau Danner, she was the same. Not a bundle of laughs, neither of them.

Well, what'd you expect? Bet you Frau Danner didn't have an easy life with that husband of hers.

Now his daughter, Barbara Spangler, she's a real looker, but made in the same mould as her parents.

Oh yes, I know the rumours about the Danners, how they keep everything in the family, even their children. Who doesn't know what folk say?

And being a postman you get told this and that, but if you was always to believe everything you hear...

Tell you what, I couldn't care less who fathered Barbara's two kids.

I'd have my hands full if I stopped to bother with other folks' business. No good asking me, you'll have to try someone else. I deliver the post and I keep well out of the rest of it.

The weather has been rather better all day than for the last few weeks. No more snow, and the wind has died down. Now and then a few drops of rain fall. There's a milky white veil over the landscape. Mist, typical for this time of year. The first swathes of it are drifting over from the outskirts of the woods towards the meadow and the house. It's late afternoon, and the day will soon be coming to an end. Dusk is slowly gathering.

He walks towards the house. The post is stuck between the metal bars over the window beside the front door. If there's no one at home, the postman always leaves the post here. It meant they didn't need a letter-box. And it's only occasionally that there's no one at all at home on the farm. Usually someone is there to take the post in, and if not, then there's the window next to the door.

A newspaper is stuck between the two bars and the window pane, that's all. He puts it under his arm, takes the front-door key out of his jacket pocket. A large, heavy, old-fashioned key made of iron. It shines blue-black with much use over the years. He puts the key in the lock and opens the door of the house.

When he has unlocked the door, stale and slightly musty-smelling air meets him. Just before entering the house he turns and looks in all directions. He goes in, locking the door again after him.

He follows the corridor through the house to the kitchen. Opens the kitchen door and goes in. Gets the fire in the stove going with the wood left over from this morning. Fills the steamer with potatoes just as he did first thing today. Feeds the animals and gives them water. Milks the cows and sees to the calves.

This time, however, he doesn't leave the house as soon as he has finished work in the cowshed. He goes out to the barn, takes the pickaxe he has left there ready, and tries to dig a hole in the floor at the right-hand corner of the barn.

He loosens the trodden mud floor with the pickaxe. But just under the surface he meets stony, rocky ground. He tries in another place. No luck there either. He gives up his plan.

Treads down the loose earth again and scatters straw over it.

He goes back to the kitchen. Hungry after his strenuous work, he cuts himself a piece of smoked meat in the larder. Takes the last of the bread from the kitchen cupboard. A sip of water from the tap, and he leaves the kitchen and the house.

Kurt Huber,
mechanic, aged 21

It was on the Tuesday, yes, that's right, Tuesday 22 March 195...

Old Danner, he'd phoned us at the firm a week before, said it was very urgent.

But it wasn't the sort of weather when you'd want to spend forty-five minutes cycling out there. It kept on snowing, raining too now and then. Filthy weather, it was. And we had plenty of work on hand in the firm.

I'll tell you straight, I don't like going out to those people at Tannöd.

Why not? Well, they're kind of funny. Loners. And tight-fisted too. So mean they'd grudge you every bit of bread, every sip of water.

I'd had to go out there to repair the engine of the machine that slices roots for animal feed once already, that was last summer, and they didn't even offer me a snack when I took my break. Even though I'd been working away on that engine for over five hours, screwing and unscrewing parts. Not so much as a glass of water or a cup of milk, never mind a beer.

But then again, to be honest, I couldn't have swallowed a drop they gave me. The whole place was so grubby, really mucky. I can't stand that kind of thing.

When I washed my hands at the tap in the kitchen I took a closer look around the room. I mean, how can anyone live like that? I couldn't, not me.

Old Frau Danner in her mended, dirty apron. Her little grandson, always with a snotty nose.

You'd think she might have wiped the child's nose for him. The little boy was crawling about on the kitchen floor, picking something up now and then and putting it straight in his mouth. Old Frau Danner saw him do it and never said a thing. When the little boy started crying the old woman put him on her lap and gave him his dummy. She'd licked the dummy first and dipped it in the sugar bowl standing on the table. Licked it and then dipped it in the sugar. Can you imagine that? It was all sticky, the bowl was crusty with spit and sugar.

I mean, I can't understand it. I really couldn't have swallowed a morsel, but they might have offered me something all the same, if you ask me it's the thing to do. Only right and proper, wouldn't you say?

Well, so when I was told to go and repair the engine, I wasn't all that keen on cycling out there again. In such weather, at that.

Then old Danner made another phone call, complained to the boss, so there was nothing for it, I had to go. I set out to cycle there around eight a.m. on the Tuesday, after I'd picked my tools up from the firm.

When did I get there? Oh, around nine, I guess that was it. Yes, just before nine, round about then. I was sweating by the time I reached their farm. I went right ahead through the garden gate and up to the front door, but the door was locked. First it's so urgent, they're in a tearing hurry, I said to myself, and then there's no one in. Oh well, maybe they're round behind the house.

So I pushed my bike round the farmyard. On the way I passed the two windows of the sheds on the back of the house. And I looked in through one of the windows. Couldn't make out anything, though. I mean, one of them could have been in the cowshed with the cattle. But no one was. I looked through the kitchen window as well. Still didn't see anyone.

Then I didn't really know what to do. So I leaned my bike up against a fruit tree and waited.

How long did I wait? Oh, it must have been about ten minutes, I'd say. I lit a cigarette and smoked it. That takes around ten minutes.

Someone ought to come along soon, I thought to myself. And after a while I did see someone. Don't know if it was a man or a woman. Some way off, standing in the fields out there.

At first I thought, ah, there comes old Danner now.

I called and I whistled. But whoever it was in the fields didn't hear. The figure didn't come any closer, disappeared as suddenly as it had come.

I waited a while longer. I was feeling a right charlie. Didn't want to cycle home without repairing the engine neither. I'd only have to go out there again in a couple of days' time. An engine like that isn't going to repair itself, is it?

So there was nothing for it, I went to the shack where they kept the machine. It's round behind the barn, or rather behind the barn and the cowshed, they're built right next to each other.

I knew where to find the root-slicing machine from last time.

How late was it then? Oh, around nine-thirty. Yes, the time would have been nine-thirty.

The door had a padlock on it. I looked around to see if I could find the key to the padlock anywhere.

Some people hide keys very close, you see. For instance under a stone or a bucket, or on a hook at the side of a building just under the overhang of the roof. You wouldn't believe the things I've seen. They do it so they won't mislay the key and it'll be easier to find. It's daft, it's downright irresponsible. Might as well leave their doors wide open. But that's how some folk are. It really makes you wonder.

But the Danners hadn't left the key anywhere, not under a stone nor hanging from a hook. My bad luck. I wanted to go home, like I said, but not without doing the job first, and my next job for a customer wasn't until the afternoon, that was for the Brunners over in Einhausen.

So on impulse I fetched my toolbox from the carrier of the bike. I took out a pair of pliers and very carefully bent aside the little wire the padlock was hanging from. That way I just had to take the padlock off.

I felt like a housebreaker or a thief. But

there you are, I didn't want to cycle out again, and if anyone had come along I could have explained.

No one did come along, though. There was only the dog, I heard it barking its head off. Didn't see it anywhere, though. You could hear the cows mooing too. Not loud but all the time, I remember that now.

When I'd taken the padlock off and opened the shack door, I could finally fix the machine. I'd already wasted a whole hour as it was. No one pays you for wasted time, certainly not a penny-pincher like old Danner.

A man like that, he watches every minute, anyone would think it was *you* that owed *him* something, he'll starve to death yet with a bit of bread in his mouth. It was the cylinder-head gasket had gone, I'd thought that was the trouble all along. Changing one of those takes time. Back in summer I'd already told old Danner he wanted to buy a new machine, we'd take the old one in part-payment. It was a pre-war model at that, but no, the old skinflint didn't want to, even though that's the usual thing to do these days.

There still wasn't a soul in sight at the farm. I was getting to feel the whole thing was eerie. So I left the door of the shack where they kept the root-slicing machine open. First, that gave me more light to work by, and second anyone could see straight off that I was busy repairing the engine.

I'd almost finished, was just about to screw one last nut back in place when it slips clean through my fingers and rolls towards the cistern.

There was this old cistern in the shack, for keeping milk cool. You stood the full milk churns in it. Thank God there wasn't any water in the cistern, it was empty.

So down I climb into the cistern. It's not deep, comes maybe up to my thighs if that, and I fish out my nut.

At the very moment I was bending down to feel around for the nut, I thought a shadow scurried past. I couldn't see it, it was more of a feeling. A voice inside you saying look, there's someone there, even if you can't see whoever it is. But it's there, you feel it, there's somebody there.

So I'm up and out of the cistern in a flash.

'Hey, anyone there? Hello!' I shouted.

No answer, though. I'd not been feeling too comfortable before, now the farm seemed downright uncanny. And the dog barking and barking all the time, though I couldn't see it.

So I screwed the nut on as fast as I could and packed up my tools. Now to give the engine a trial run, and then I'd be off double quick.

I fitted the padlock back where it was before. Put my stuff on the bike and set off through the middle of the farmyard.

As I was pushing the bike around the house, there still wasn't a soul in sight. But the door of the old machinery shed was open, and it hadn't been open before. I'm certain of that.

So I think to myself, maybe there's someone there after all. And I leave my bike again and go a few steps over to the shed.

'Hello, anyone there?' I called, but no answer this time either. Nothing.

I didn't want to go any further into the shed, it somehow didn't seem right to me.

I went to the front door of the house again and shook it, but, like I said, it was locked.

Nothing would have kept me at that farm any longer. I was glad to get away from the place.

I must have finished the repair just after two, because on the way back to the village I heard the church clock strike the half-hour.

Did I see anyone else in the fields? No, not a soul. Only a couple of crows. No wonder in that weather. It had started raining again, a light drizzle. I cycled as if the Devil himself was after me.

All the way back from the farm I kept thinking: suppose there really was someone there, he'd have been bound to hear the sound of the engine's trial run, couldn't miss it.

I must have been wrong, there wasn't anyone there, but that shadow, the voice inside me, the odd feeling, well, I don't know.

When I got to my next job in Einhausen, I told them the story, because I couldn't get it out of my head.

I'd been over five hours at the Danner farm in Tannöd, and no one came along. Five hours alone at that farm without setting eyes on a living soul.

Frau Brunner in Einhausen thought it was very strange too. 'If only because of the little boy they have there. A child like that has to sleep, has to eat something,' she said. 'You can't just go wandering about like gypsies, not with a small child.'

But all her husband said was, 'They'll be getting in wood, that takes time.'

The knife. Where's the knife, his pocket-knife? He always has it on him, in his back trouser pocket. It's been a fixed habit since the day he was first given that knife.

He can still remember every detail, he got it the day he was confirmed. A present from his sponsor at his confirmation. A clasp-knife, a beautiful, useful knife with a brown handle. It was in a box. He remembers every detail.

He remembers the gift paper wrapping of the box. Thin tissue paper printed with flowers, garden flowers in bright colours. And the package was done up with a red bow. He was so eager to undo it he tore the paper. A brown cardboard box came into sight. His hands trembled with excitement and delight as he opened that box. And there it lay, a pocket-knife. His pocket-knife. From that day on, he proudly took the knife around with him the whole time. It was his most precious possession.

None of the other village boys had a knife like that. He still sensed the good feeling he had when he took the knife in his hand, or just had it somewhere on him. He often liked to hold it, passing it from one hand to the other. It gave him a sense of security. Yes, security.

Over the years, the knife became worn with much use. But the feeling stayed with him.

And now he's been looking for the knife all day. When did he last use it? Where had he left it?

He goes through this last day again in his mind. Slowly, as if emerging from the mist, a picture comes before his eyes. He sees himself, knife in hand, cutting off a piece of smoked meat. Sees himself putting the pocket-knife down beside the plate with the meat on it.

He feels uneasiness rise slowly inside him. His heart is racing, his heart's in his mouth. He didn't put the knife back in his pocket. He was sure of that. He left the knife there. His knife. His knife is lying in the larder next to the smoked meat. He sees it there in his mind's eye quite clearly. He feels he only has to reach for it.

Panic seizes him. He must go back to the house. He must retrieve the knife, his knife. He can't wait until evening, can't wait for nightfall. That will be hours, it will be too long. So much can happen before evening.

Why didn't he think of that this morning? He was feeding the animals, he was in a hurry. He left without checking that everything was back in its proper place. That was his mistake. Why didn't he think of it until now? Never mind that, there's nothing for it, he must go to the house. He must run the risk of entering the place in broad daylight.

He sees the bicycle leaning against a fruit tree. Sees the open door of the shack where they keep the root-slicing machine. He hears someone humming, whistling. Cautiously, he comes closer to the shack. He peers in. The man is so busy repairing the machine that he doesn't notice him. From where he lurks by the door he watches the unknown man.

Something drops from the man's hand, falls on the floor, rolls over the ground and into the cistern. The stranger curses, looks searchingly around. Finally he climbs into the cistern.

This is the moment he's been waiting for. He hurries past the open door. He's already round the corner of the house before the other man can climb out of the cistern. Takes the key out of his jacket pocket and disappears through the door. The pocket-knife is lying right where he left it. He waits a few more minutes. They seem to him like an eternity. He wants to wait for a good moment to leave the house again. The engine of the root-slicing machine begins turning over. He hears the noise. Quickly, he leaves the house without being seen.

Dagmar,
daughter of Johann Sterzer, aged 20

It was that Tuesday, about two-thirty. We'd just gone out into the garden, me and my mother. To tidy up the beds.

As soon as we're out in the garden, the mechanic from the agricultural machinery firm comes by on his bike. I know him, he came here once to repair one of our machines.

He braked right by our garden fence. Stopped but didn't get off his bike. He just called to us from the fence, said if we saw Danner to tell him his machine was working fine again. It took him five hours, he said, he'd be sending the invoice in the post.

Then the mechanic got back on his bike and rode away.

My mother and I were surprised to hear there wasn't anyone at the Danner farm. But it didn't bother us. A little later I was thinking no more about it. I'd forgotten it entirely.

About an hour after the mechanic came by, young
Hansl Hauer turned up. I was still in the garden
with my mother. Hansl was waving his arms in the
air. Waving them about like crazy. He was all
worked up. Long before he got to us he was shouting, asking if Father was at home, saying something had happened at the Danner place.

At that very moment Father came out of the
front door. He'd seen Hansl through the window.

Hansl still hadn't reached us when he started
shouting again. His dad had sent him, he said,
because there was something wrong up at the
Danners'.

'Herr Sterzer, he wants you to go up to Tannöd
and the farm too,' he told my father.

At Hauer's, they didn't want to go poking about
there on their own. None of them had seen the
Danners since Saturday, he said. Even on Sunday
there wasn't a single one of the Danner family at
church.

Then I remembered what the mechanic said, how
he too had told us there wasn't anyone at home at
the Danner farm.

Hansl told us his aunt had sent him up to the
Danners' place. To look around, because no one at
the Hauer farm had seen any of them for the last
few days.

66

The cattle were mooing in the farmyard, he said, and the dog was whining frantically. Hansl shook the front door of the house, but it was locked. He shook it really hard, he knocked too, and called to Barbara and Marianne. And when no one answered, and all of a sudden he didn't like the way it felt up there at the farm, he went back to his dad.

He told him all about it, and his dad sent him over to us, for one of us to go up to the farm with him too. So now Hansl was here with Father and Lois, they were to go straight up to Tannöd with him, and Hauer would be waiting for them there.

Father set off right away with Lois. Up to the Danner farm. They took Hansl with them.

And that's where they found them. All of them.

By Thy willing obedience,
deliver them, O Lord!
By the endless love of Thy divine heart,
deliver them, O Lord!
By Thy anguish and Thy labour,
deliver them, O Lord!
By Thy blood and sweat,
deliver them, O Lord!
By Thy captivity,
deliver them, O Lord!
By Thy cruel scourging,
deliver them, O Lord!
By Thy shameful crown of thorns,
deliver them, O Lord!
By Thy toil and labour in carrying the Cross,
deliver them, O Lord!
By the precious blood of Thy wounds,
deliver them, O Lord!
By Thy bitter Cross and Passion,
deliver them, O Lord!
By Thy death and burial,
deliver them, O Lord!
By Thy holy Resurrection,
deliver them, O Lord!
By Thy miraculous Ascension,
deliver them, O Lord!

By the coming of the Holy Ghost, the Comforter,
deliver them, O Lord!
On the Day of Judgement
deliver them, O Lord!
Miserable sinners that we are,
we beg You, hear our prayer!
Thou who forgavest the sinner Mary Magdalene,
we beg You, hear our prayer!

Michael Baumgartner trudges towards the Tannöd farm through the sleet. The wind is blowing into his face. He knows the way, he knows the property. Otherwise it would have been tricky, finding the farm in the middle of the night, in this weather. He's worked there quite often over the years. In the woods in spring, in the fields in summer. Always plenty of work going on the Danner farm.

Mick, as he's generally known, doesn't fancy working too long on any one farm. He moves from place to place, 'always on the road', as he says. Sometimes he sleeps in a barn, sometimes in a loft.

He makes his living, or so everyone thinks, from casual labour. Now and then he's been on the roads as a pedlar too.

In fact, however, he lives mainly by theft, breaking and entering, taking his chance to commit minor criminal offences.

He takes a good look around the farms where he works. By the time he moves on again, he usually knows plenty about them. What's to be had where and who from. Mick can use this trick to manipulate people. He has a natural talent, 'a bent for it' is the way he puts it.

He'll work at a farm for a time. He works hard, too, that's how to win the trust of the farming folk. Flatters them, says how well a man 'keeps his place going', tells him 'what a fine farm this is', cracks a joke or two with a twinkle in his eye, and the proud owner of the farm will start bragging. Even if he's usually buttoned up, perhaps most of all if he's usually buttoned up. Mick keeps his ears and eyes open, and after a while he goes on his way. He passes on what he knows about the farms and their owners, or if a good opportunity offers he may seize it himself. Whatever suits him best.

If you go about it cleverly, if you're not too greedy and you can bide your time, you can usually get by pretty well. You don't want to let yourself get caught, but only the greedy, the careless and those who go too far are caught.

Mick's not greedy, it's not in his nature, and he has all the time in the world.

And his brother-in-law disposes of the stolen goods. His sister and her husband have a little farm in Unterwald, ideally situated. Out of the way, difficult to spot.

His brother-in-law did very well out of the black market just after the war. With the currency reform on 20 June 1948, that kind of trade died a natural death.

But during his time as a black marketeer the brother-in-law managed to build up good contacts. A little ring of receivers, traders and petty criminals got together.

Now their functions are distinct. Mick goes from farm to farm, picking up information. When the right time comes he, his brother-in-law or one of his brother-in-law's old mates will break into the place. Steal money, clothes, jewellery, food, anything that can be turned into cash. No one ever thinks of connecting him, Mick, with the burglary. It's too long since he let whatever farmer is the victim set eyes on him.

If it gets too hot for him in one place, he moves on to another. Or takes a break. Shifts his business interests into other areas.

Working as a pedlar was a good one.

His brother-in-law was on the road as a pedlar before and even during the war years. Used to sell the country people all kinds of stuff: shoelaces, hair lotion, real coffee before the war, ersatz coffee in wartime. All manner of other bits and pieces. A leg injury kept him out of the forces. 'Old Adolf needed men, not cripples. He could make cripples of them himself', he always used to say, laughing and clapping his thigh.

Even now, with the end of the black market trade, he, the brother-in-law, goes around on the road with his wares every so often.

At first Mick went with him. Now he sometimes goes on the road selling stuff himself. But only occasionally.

He much prefers working on the land as a casual labourer, finding out about the farmers and their properties.

Late last summer he worked as a picker during the hop harvest for a while. The pay wasn't bad, and nor was the food. Even the pickers' sleeping quarters in a barn had been to his liking.

In autumn he went from house to house as a pedlar for a short time. He even passed Tannöd, but he didn't let them see him at Danner's farm. He didn't want to be spotted, because the Tannöd folk were still on his list. For a rainy day. Something in reserve, you might say.

There are no flies on Mick. You want to save up some of your best opportunities for times of need, like keeping your savings in a stocking. And Danner is a nice fat stocking full of savings, Mick knows that for certain.

November didn't go so well for him. He and his brother-in-law were planning to sell on some copper wire.

Copper was still in great demand, always had been, fetched a good price if you knew the right dealers. His brother-in-law knew a couple of blokes who cut the overhead wires of telephone lines. Then the wires could be sold on. The two blokes weren't all that bright, the whole plan flopped, and for the first time ever Mick found himself spending a few weeks in jail for receiving and a few other minor offences.

Not a lengthy sentence, but it was three months all the same. He hasn't been free all that long yet. He can't go to his sister's. His brother-in-law is still in jail, and his sister can't be doing with another mouth to feed. So this is the right time to go to his stocking full of savings. The Tannöd farmer is ripe for the plucking.

He knows the farm well from his previous visits. Old Danner once took him round the whole house and farm. It was pure joy to hear him showing off about 'his place'!

The old fool had even told him about his money, adding that he 'didn't put it all in the bank', not he. He always had something in the house, he said, plenty to be going on with. They'd been great cronies back then. He knew just how to cosy up to Danner.

The old man was crafty, but Mick could handle him. Danner boasted of how he'd outwitted his neighbours, of the times he'd taken them for a ride.

He talked and talked, and soon Mick had the farmer where he wanted him. That's why he's on his way to the farm now, in the middle of the night. He wasn't reckoning on such lousy weather, though. He's already drenched to the skin when he finally reaches the farm. He knows his way about the property. Even the dog is no problem. When he was on the road he once lodged with a shepherd who taught him how to handle dogs. And the animal still knows him from his time at the farm.

He gets into the barn from the old machinery shed, and then up into the loft. Dead easy. Everything went without a hitch. No one saw him in the darkness. The dog knew him and didn't start barking. He fastens a rope to a beam in the suspended ceiling of the barn as an emergency exit. Better safe than sorry. After that he puts straw on the floor-boards above the suspended ceiling to muffle his footsteps. He doesn't want to wake the sleeping family in the house below. He doesn't want anyone to notice his presence. This is Friday. The sun will rise in a few hours' time. From up here he can watch the farmyard, seize his moment to get into the house and plunder the piggy-bank. He's satisfied. Moving fast is always a bad idea in his line of work. More haste, less speed, as they say. No one will find him up here. From inside the loft he can push the roof-tiles a little way apart to get a view of the whole farmyard. He can wait. He has plenty of time.

Georg Hauer,
farmer, aged 49

Friday March the eighteenth, that's when I last saw Danner.

I was planning to go over to Einhausen that day.

Had to fetch something from the ironmonger's there. I'm going to rebuild my barn this year, that's why I took the cart and drove.

On foot it takes you a good hour, I'd say.

When I'm just past Danner's property — the road there runs by the farm — the old man waves to me. He was some way off.

Since that business with Barbara I've always tended to avoid Danner. We haven't talked to each other much since. But I stopped the cart all the same. Reluctantly.

'Hold on a minute there! I want to ask you something,' the old man called.

First he just hummed and hawed. I was starting to wish I hadn't stopped at all. Suddenly he asks me if I'd seen anything, if I'd noticed anything.

'What was there to notice? I haven't seen any-thing out of the ordinary.' I was getting really annoyed with myself for stopping by now.

If he was going on at me like that, it meant he had something or other in mind. A sly fox, old Danner was. You had to watch your step with him. So I was surprised when all he asked was had anyone met me, had I seen anyone?

'Why?' I asked back.

'There was someone tried to break into our house last night. Nothing stolen, but the lock's been wrenched off the machinery shed.'

'Better call the police,' I told him.

But he wouldn't have the police in the house, he told me.

'Don't want nothing to do with the cops.'

He'd searched the whole place, he said. Went up to the loft too, took a lamp and shone it in all the corners, but he didn't find anything.

All the same, he said, all last night he thought he heard someone in the loft. So he went up there first thing in the morning. But he didn't find anything, and nothing was missing.

I asked him if he'd like me to help him search. Pig-headed like he was, all he said was the fellow would have made off by now. Only he didn't know how, because all the footprints you could see just led to the house and not away.

Fresh snow had fallen overnight. Not much, just a thin covering. But he'd been able to make out some of the footprints well enough.

'Want me to bring my revolver?' I asked. I still have one at home, left over from the war.

But Danner wouldn't have that.

'No need. I've got a gun myself and a good stout stick. I'll soon send the fellow packing.'

I offered again to look in at his place on my way home, help him search the farmyard again.

But the stubborn old sod said no.

Then, just as I'm about to go on in the cart, the old man turns round again and says, 'And the stupid thing is I mislaid the front-door key yesterday. If you find a key on the road, a key that long' — and he showed me the length of the key with his hands — 'then it's mine.'

That was the end of the conversation, and I went on. I really did mean to look in on Danner again on my way back.

But the weather got worse, it was raining, there was even a bit of snow, so I went straight home.

There was a frost that night too. Spring just didn't want to come this year.

I noticed none of the Danners were at church on Sunday, but I thought nothing much of that.

Then on Monday I was out in the fields near the woods. My fields there march side by side with Danner's land. I was ploughing. Didn't see any of the Danners the whole time, though.

But Tuesday, my sister-in-law Anna sent young Hansl up to their farm to take a look around. It wasn't till then I remembered all that about the break-in and the missing front-door key. And you know the rest of it.

Old Frau Danner is sitting at the kitchen table, praying:
'Gentle Jesus, meek and mild, Thou art our salvation,
Thou alone art our life, our resurrection.
I therefore pray Thee
do not abandon me in my hour of need,
but for the sake of Thy most sacred heart's struggle with
    death,
and for the sake of Thy immaculate mother's pain,
come to the aid of Thy servants,
whom Thou hast redeemed with Thy precious blood.'

She holds her old, well-worn prayer book. She is alone, alone with herself and her thoughts.

Barbara is out in the cowshed, taking a last look at the cattle. Her husband is already in bed. Like the children and the new maid.

She treasures this time of the evening as the most precious thing she has. She sits in the kitchen with *The*

Myrtle Wreath in her hands. The prayer book is worn and shabby now. Back then, many years ago, a whole lifetime ago, she was given *The Myrtle Wreath. A spiritual guide for brides* for her wedding day, according to the custom of the time. A book of devotions for Christian women.

Who knows, could she have lived this life without the grace and comfort of God and the Mother of God? A life full of humiliations, indignities and blows. Only the comfort she found in her faith kept her going. Kept her going all these years. Who could she have confided in? Her mother died during the First World War. So did her father soon afterwards, at the time when her future husband came to the farm to work as a labourer.

When he arrived, it was the first time anyone had ever paid her a little attention. That attention was balm to her soul. Her whole life up to now had been ruled by work and her parents' deep religious faith.

She grew up in cold, sanctimonious surroundings. No tenderness, no loving embraces to warm her soul, not a kind word. The life she led was marked by the rhythm of the seasons and the work on the farm that went with them, and by her parents' life within the boundaries of their stern faith.

Such spiritual narrowness of mind could be felt almost physically.

Then the man who would be her husband came to the farm as a labourer. She, who had never been particularly pretty, was now desired by this good-looking man. From the first she knew in her heart of hearts that she herself, a nondescript little woman and already fading, was not the true object of his desire. Still unmarried, she was an old maid at thirty-two. He was tall and well-built, and not yet twenty-seven. But she closed her eyes to the fact that he wanted the farm, not her body.

Against her better judgement she agreed to marry him. He changed soon after the wedding. Showed his true nature. Was uncivil, insulted her, even hit her when she didn't do as he wanted.

She took it all without complaint. No one could understand it, but she loved her husband, loved him even when he beat her. She was dependent on every word he spoke, everything he did. Never mind how rough and hardhearted he proved to be.

When she was expecting her child, his brutality was hard to bear. He humiliated her in every possible way. Cheated on her openly, before all eyes, with the maid they had at the farm then. That was the first time she had to move out of the marital bedroom and into a smaller one because another woman had taken her place. She was enslaved by him, subjected, in bondage to him. For the rest of her life.

Her daughter Barbara was born in the fields at potato-harvesting time.

He didn't even allow the heavily pregnant mother the privilege of a confinement in her own bed. On the morning when she felt the first contractions he made her go out into the fields with the others. She was bent double with pain, and when blood was already running down her legs, and the child was fighting its determined way out of her body with all its might, she gave birth to the little creature at the side of the field. Brought her into the world there under the open sky. He forced her to go on working in the days after she gave birth too. She had no peace.

The maid left, and she moved back into her bedroom. She let him have his way with her again. Without complaint. She couldn't help it.

Maids came and went. Few of them stayed long. As time passed her husband calmed down, or so she thought. She was resigned to her fate.

Her daughter Barbara grew up. She adored her father, and he showed her great love and tenderness. She was twelve when her father first raped her. It took the mother some time to see the change in her daughter.

She didn't want to notice the abuse of her own child. Didn't want to acknowledge it. Was too weak to leave her husband, and where could she have gone? His conduct had one advantage: it meant that he lost interest in her entirely.

The more his daughter grew to womanhood, the less he wanted to sleep with his wife. She was perfectly happy with that state of affairs.

So she kept quiet. Her husband could do as he pleased, he never met with any resistance.

Except once, when the little Polish girl was here on the farm, assigned to them as a foreign worker. The girl got away from him. The way she did it was barred to his wife.

She had lived a hard life. A life full of deprivation and indignity, but she couldn't give it up. She must tread the path to the end, she would empty the bitter goblet to the dregs. She knew that. It was the trial that the Lord had laid upon her.

Funny, that Polish girl has come back into her mind several times today, flitting through her memory like a shadow. She hadn't thought of the foreign worker for years. The old woman puts her prayer book down.

She looks through the window into the dark, stormy night.

Her husband has spent all day searching for whatever ne'er-do-well tried to break into the farm yesterday. She heard footsteps last night. As if someone were haunting the place.

Her husband found nothing, and he had been calm enough all day.

'The fellow will have made off again', he told them. 'There's nothing missing, I searched everywhere. I'll shut the dog up in the barn tonight, no one gets past the dog. And I'll have my gun beside my bed.'

That had reassured them all. She felt safe, just as she had felt safe on this farm all her life.

Barbara said she was going out to the cowshed again, 'to see the cattle are all right.'

Where can Barbara be? She ought to have been back long ago. She'll go and look for her.

Moving laboriously, she gets up from the table. She takes her prayer book and puts it on the kitchen dresser. And goes out, over to the cowshed.

Old Danner tosses and turns restlessly in bed. He can't get to sleep tonight.

He tries to, but the wind, constantly whistling through the cracks in the window frame, gives him no peace.

He's turned the whole house upside down today. He can't get those footprints out of his mind. Footprints leading to the house. He could see them clearly in the newly fallen snow this morning, before the rain washed them away.

He looked in every nook and cranny of the house. Didn't find anything. He's sure no one can hide from him on his own property. This is his domain.

He's repaired the lock on the machinery shed. The fellow must have gone around the house and made off in the direction of the woods. He can only have gone that way. Otherwise he, Danner, would have found more tracks.

In the evening he searched the whole property again. In the process he noticed that the light bulb in the cowshed had gone. He'll have to get a new one. Until then they'll just have to make do as best they can with the old oil lamps.

The new maid looks as if she'd be a good hard worker. That's what he needs. He can't be doing with anyone who's work-shy. The farm is too much for him and Barbara on their own. During the summer, anyway.

In winter they get by somehow.

It's harder and harder to find labourers and maids to work on the land these days. Most of them try their luck in town. Lured there by better pay and lighter work.

Town life, that's not for him. He has to feel free. Be his own master. No one tells him what to do. He decides on everything here. On this farm he is Lord God Almighty, never mind how much his wife prays. The older she grows the more pious she gets.

What's keeping the old woman in the kitchen so long? Sits praying under that crucifix half the night, wasting expensive electric light.

He'll have to get up and go and see.

In his stockinged feet, clad only in his nightshirt and a pair of long johns, he slips his wooden clogs on. Shuffles down the stone flags of the corridor to the kitchen.

The door of the room next to it is open.

What the hell's the idea? What are those women doing in the cowshed at this time of night? You had to see to everything yourself around here.

Much annoyed, he goes into the room next to the kitchen and then on, over to the cowshed.

From his vantage point, Mick has been watching the comings and goings on the farm all day long

He sees old Danner finding traces of the break-in. It's dead easy to keep out of the old man's way.

Old Danner searches the whole place. He even climbs up to Mick's hide-out in the loft.

Mick holds his breath. Stands there with one hand gripping the knife in his pocket. Hiding by the chimney, behind the farmer's back. He could touch his shoulder. Danner is perched on the steps up to the loft not an arm's length away from him. Trying to light up the dark loft with his lamp, which is very faint.

He doesn't notice the straw scattered over the suspended ceiling of the barn, or the rope hanging ready.

Mick waits all day. He can take his time. He knows just where the Tannöd farmer hides his money. He's planned everything out down to the smallest detail.

If it all goes as he's calculated, he can leave the house unseen. And if not?

Mick shrugs off this idea. He doesn't shrink from using violence. Violence is part of his job. He'll play it by ear.

As evening comes on, two more strangers appear in the farmyard. Two women going towards the house in the rain. They knock. Both of them are let in. After about an hour the women come out of the house again. They say goodbye to each other, and one of them goes back indoors.

Hansl Hauer,
aged 13, Georg Hauer's son

It was the Tuesday when my auntie told me to go over to the Danner farm.

'No one's seen or heard anything of them over there,' she told me. 'Maybe something's happened and they need help.'

So I went over.

I guess it was about three. But I'm not sure.

There wasn't any of them in the farmyard, so I knocked at the front door. I knocked good and loud, I shook the door, but it was locked and nobody opened it.

So then I went round the house. Peered in at all the windows. Couldn't see a thing, though. The place looked quite empty. Like there wasn't anybody there.

I heard the dog. Whining terribly, it was. And I heard the cattle in the cowshed. The cows were lowing like anything. But I couldn't get into the cowshed, it was locked from inside.

You can get into the cowshed from the old machinery shed, though, I know that. First you go through the barn, then there's a wooden door into the cowshed on the left.

And the door of the machinery shed was standing open. Wide open, but I didn't fancy going in there.

I just stood at the door and called. I called for Barbara and Marianne. But there wasn't any answer and I didn't want to go in. I was too scared because the cattle were bellowing like that, and everything was all different from usual. Like as if the place was deserted.

I got gooseflesh, I really did, it seemed so scary.

Something's wrong, that's what I kept on thinking. I felt like there was a bell ringing in my head. Same as an alarm bell when the fire engine's coming out. So I ran home quick, I told my auntie and my dad.

Dad said I was to fetch Farmer Sterzer, because he wasn't going over to that farm on his own.

So I went on, over to the Sterzers in Upper Tannöd.

Farmer Sterzer's Dagmar was outside in the garden with her mother. Working on the garden beds.

I shouted to them way before I got there, I was in such a state. Asked if Farmer Sterzer was home, and he came out of the door right that moment. I told him there was something wrong up at the Danner place. No one was in, and the dog was whining and all that, and the cattle lowing in the shed. And I said my dad said to fetch him to go over there with my dad. Because my dad didn't want to go alone.

So Farmer Sterzer called Alois right away. Lois is the farm-hand at the Sterzer place, he's going to marry Dagmar.

Then I went over to Tannöd and the Danner farm with Farmer Sterzer and Lois.

It was just before we reached the house we met my dad. He'd been waiting for Farmer Sterzer there. Then he went on up to the Danner farm with us.

And then we found them.

Well, not me, because my dad wouldn't let me go into the house. He said I was to stay outside.

And after Farmer Sterzer and Lois came out of the barn again, white as chalk they were, I was really glad I hadn't gone in with them.

My dad told me to go down to the village. 'And tell them they'd better call the police from the mayor's house.' So that's what I did.

I fetched my bike and went over to the village, I went to the mayor's, and I shouted out how they were all dead at Danner's. All of them murdered dead. I shouted it in everyone's face, even the mayor's.

Johann Sterzer,
aged 52, farmer in Upper Tannöd

I was sitting in the living-room. I saw young Hansl through the window. He was waving his arms about, and he kept on shouting something.

Right away, I guessed something had happened, but I thought it must be at the Hauer place.

So I came straight out of the house. Hansl says to me, 'Dad sent me because there's nothing stirring at the Danners'.'

He, that's Hansl, he'd been to look around on their farm today, he said, and there wasn't anyone at home and the dog was whining terribly. And the cattle were restless too.

'But Dad doesn't fancy going there alone,' he told me, so I called Alois and we went over to the Tannöd farm with Hansl.

I'd noticed myself there was nothing stirring there. When I was ploughing on Saturday, in the field next to Danner's land, I didn't see anyone all the time.

It was odd, yes, but I thought no more of it.

They'll be in the woods, that's all it is, I thought to myself.

Hauer was waiting for us just before we got to the house. We all went up to the farmyard together. I saw at once that the door of the machinery shed was open.

Hauer knows his way around the farm since that business with Barbara. He was in and out of the place a lot back then.

'We can get into the barn through the shed. There's a door into the cowshed from there, and we can go on into the house from the cowshed,' he said to me and Lois.

He told Hansl he'd better stay outside. That was all right by Lois and me, so it was just the three of us went into the shed. Sure enough, there was a little door there. On the back wall of the shed, but it was fastened shut with a hook or something on the other side.

I was going out again to see if there wasn't some other way into the house.

But Hauer took my sleeve. 'That door's so flimsy we can just push it in,' he says.

Lois agreed with him, so the three of us braced ourselves against that little door.

After a while, yes, it did give way, and there we were in the barn.

It was very dark inside. The only daylight came in through an open door on the left-hand side of the barn. On the right-hand side hay was stacked up, and the other stocks of feed, and there were piles of straw everywhere against the back wall and the left-hand side. But we couldn't really see much in that dark barn. It was more like guesswork.

The bellowing of the animals in the cowshed was getting louder and louder.

'There's a cow there!' Hauer saw her first. The cow was standing right in the doorway.

'Come on, come on, she must have torn herself free.'

Hauer went over to the cow in the doorway. My eyes weren't really used to the darkness in that barn yet. I didn't like it at all, but I didn't fancy being left behind on my own either. So I followed Hauer. Looked like Lois felt the same. But as he started off after Hauer he stumbled. Managed to catch himself up in time, though.

I'm about to tell Lois he'd better watch where he was going, and then I see this foot in the straw.

Lois grabbed my arm. Grabbed it tight.

We both stood there just staring at the heap of straw. We didn't neither of us move, not Lois and not me. We simply stood there.

My heart was beating like it was fit to jump right out of my chest. The ground under my feet wouldn't hold me up any more, I was so weak at the knees. I clung on to Lois with all my might, and he clung on to me.

It was all so hard to grasp, it was unspeakable.

Then Hauer pushed the straw aside. Freed them of the straw, one by one. Danner. Little Marianne, her grandma, and last of all Barbara too. They were all covered with blood. I felt such dread, I couldn't really look at them.

Everything around me was ghastly. Like in a nightmare. Like the Trud was sitting on you squeezing the air out of you. I wanted to get out of there, away from that place.

When I turned to go out, Hauer barred my way.

'We have to look for Josef,' he shouted at me. But I pushed him away. Hauer tried to keep on holding me. 'We have to look for the little boy. Where's the boy? Where's Josef?'

But I just left him standing there, I went out into the open air. So as I could breathe.

Out there I found Lois outside the machinery

shed. He was pale as a ghost. Couldn't even keep on his legs any more. He'd slid down to the ground outside the shed with his back to the wall. I sat down beside him.

But Hauer — he'd followed me out of the barn — he kept on at us. We must try to get into the house from the barn, he said.

I couldn't do any more, I was exhausted and trembling all over. I felt unspeakably awful.

Hauer still wouldn't let it go. He kept on at us, badgering us the whole time.

'We have to get inside the house. We have to find out what happened.' He kept on and on saying it. Lois and me, though, we just stayed there sitting on the ground. So in the end Hauer went back into the barn alone.

From there, so he told us later, he went on through the cowshed into the farmhouse.

A few minutes later we heard the door of the house being unlocked.

Meanwhile we'd pulled ourselves together enough to feel we could stand on our feet.

Hauer called to us again to go into the house with him. And now that we didn't have to go through the barn and past all the dead family, we finally did as he wanted and went into the house with him.

There was still a glass standing on the kitchen table. It looked like the family had only just left the room. Like one of them would come back into the kitchen any moment.

We looked around the room. The door to the little room next to it was ajar. Hauer threw the door wide. We found a woman's dead body, it was half covered by a quilt. There was blood all over the place around her.

I didn't know the woman, I'd never seen her before in my life.

Still Hauer kept on urging us to search the other rooms in the house.

And at last we found little Josef in his cot in the bedroom. He was dead too.

Alois Huber, aged 25

Supposing I hadn't stumbled, maybe we wouldn't have found them so soon — who knows? There was no light to speak of in that barn. The daylight coming in through the open cowshed door wasn't enough to make the place any brighter.

First thing off I thought I'd fallen over a stick, a piece of wood, some largish object. It was a while before I took it in.

Me and Farmer Sterzer, we just stood there. If Hauer hadn't been there to clear the straw away, I reckon we'd have stood there for ever. I reckon we'd just have stood there unable to move.

When I saw those dead bodies I felt sick.

Not that it's that easy to upset me. I saw more than enough in the war, believe you me. Everyone who was in the war saw enough dead bodies to last them a lifetime.

But a thing like that. All of them killed stone dead.

I mean, I'd known them all, they weren't strangers, they were people you saw every day.

I couldn't look at them. I was out of that barn double quick and I threw up outside the machinery shed.

Everything else, it was like the world around me had stopped. All I still felt was that sickness. That horror. Whoever did it can't be human. Whoever did it is a devil. Can't be anyone from around here, we don't have monsters like that in these parts.

If Farmer Hauer hadn't gone on and on at us like that, I'd never have gone into the house to look for the others. Never in my life.

Farmer Hauer kept pressing us to go in, though. We followed him like lambs to the slaughter. He didn't lose his nerve. I mean, it was almost unbelievable. He didn't lose his head like us, like Farmer Sterzer and me. Everything he did, he was very calm and self-controlled. And he was the one who knew Danner and his family best. I mean, he was kind of almost like his son-in-law. Well, he was little Josef's dad, right?

In his place I could never have kept such a good grip on myself. He never lost his nerve, not for a moment. I must say I admired him a bit for that, for being so self-controlled. Almost cold-blooded, he seemed.

I've seen things in my time, back under Adolf they called us boys up at fifteen years old. They put us in uniform, gave us guns and told us to go and shoot at the enemy. The enemy. What a laugh! The enemy was old men and mothers with their children, and I was supposed to shoot at them.

I was stationed in Regensberg. The Yanks had already surrounded the whole town. We were told it had to be defended to the last man. Better dead than fall into enemy hands, they said. What a load of garbage, none of that mattered now.

This group of mothers with their children and old men, they were walking through the town. They wanted the place to surrender without a fight. Only women and children and old men, they were, the other men were all at the front or taken prisoner.

The Party top brass had already made for the hills, the filthy cowards. We even had to help them pack their cases.

They wanted to scarper for it quick, those gentlemen. They sent us kids, just kids of fifteen we were, out into the street. Told us to shoot the demonstrators. We were supposed to shoot those old men, and the mothers with their children.

So in all the confusion I scarpered too. Threw

my gun away and went down to the Danube. I hid in the cellar of a burnt-out house there. That evening I swam across the river under cover of darkness. I'm a good swimmer.

I was scared then. Terrified. I was scared to death.

I thought that was the worst thing I'd ever have to see in my life.

On the other side of the Danube, in Walch, an old woman hid me for three days. She didn't have anything for herself any more. Hid me till the Yanks came into the town.

She gave me some of her dead husband's old clothes too. Because I still had my Wehrmacht uniform on, and if the Americans caught me wearing it they'd have taken me prisoner. And the Nazis, if they'd caught me they'd have shot or hanged me out of hand for deserting, for betraying the Fatherland.

I walked home from Walch. Took me almost a week before I was finally back. The whole country seemed to be on the move after the Nazis cracked up. I saw ragged figures, dead people, hanged men.

But a horror like we saw at that farm, there's no words for it. The way they were butchered — like animals.

What kind of man could he be? I mean, it was a
monster, a lunatic.

And can you tell me, why the children too? Why
those poor little mites, I ask you? Why?

Thou who lentest Thine ear to the thief on the cross,
we beg You, hear our prayer.
Thou who fillest the elect with joy in Thy mercy,
we beg You, hear our prayer.
Thou who holdest the keys of Death and Hell,
we beg You, hear our prayer.
Thou who wouldst liberate our parents, relations and bene-
*   factors from the pains of Purgatory,*
we beg You, hear our prayer.
Thou who wouldst more particularly show mercy to those
*   souls of whom no one on Earth thinks,*
we beg You, hear our prayer.
Thou who wouldst spare and forgive them all,
we beg You, hear our prayer.
Thou who wouldst satisfy their longing for You right soon,
we beg You, hear our prayer.
Thou who wouldst take them into the company of Thine elect
*   and bless them for ever,*
we beg You, hear our prayer.

The room is bathed in faint light.

He can't tell whether the curtains are drawn or not.

He sees the room before him immersed in shimmering, milky whiteness. As if through a veil as thin as gossamer.

He sees the furniture of the room. The chest of drawers, dark brown oak, a heavy chest with three drawers. Each drawer has two brass handles. They are dulled, worn with use. You have to hold both handles of the drawers, that's the only way to pull them open. They are heavy drawers.

A picture above the chest of drawers. A guardian angel leading two children across a wooden bridge. The children walk hand in hand. A boy and a girl. A stream races under the bridge at the bottom of the picture. The guardian angel, wearing a billowing white robe, has spread its arms protectively over the children. Barefoot, the angel is leading them over the wild torrent. A mountain range casts its shadow in the background. White snow can be seen on the mountain peaks.

The picture frame is gilded, the gilt is beginning to flake

off in many places. The white of the frame beneath shows through.

He knows that the bed is on the far side of the room. With the bedside table next to it.

Both made of the same dark brown oak.

A death cross stands on the bedside table, with candle-holders to its left and right. The candles are lighted

A girl lies on the bed. Little more than a child. Her eyes closed. Her face translucent, pale. Her hair, plaited into braids, hangs far down over her shoulders. A myrtle wreath has been placed around her forehead.

Hands folded on her breast. Someone, perhaps his wife, perhaps the woman who came to lay out the body, has put a death cross into her folded hands.

The girl wears a white dress. White stockings. Her feet are in white stockings, no shoes. Her figure seems to be slowly dissolving in the light of the room.

'Look at her, oh, do look, she is an angel now.'

He hears the voice of a woman. His wife? Feels his throat tightening more and more. Notices the nausea rising gradually inside him.

'She's an angel now. Isn't she beautiful?'

The nausea almost takes his breath away.

He turns and runs to the door.

Almost tears the door off its hinges, or so it seems to him. Hurries downstairs. All he wants is to get away. Out across the fields and meadows to the woods.

There he drops to the ground. He lies with his face in the cool moss. With every breath he takes in the cold, earthy aroma of the woods. A scream rises from deep inside him. The scream makes its way out. He screams in his despair. There is nothing human about the scream, he screams in despair like a wounded animal.

The scream wakes him. He sits up in bed, bathed in sweat.

The dream is repeated night after night. Sometimes his wife is lying dead on the bed before him. On other nights the girl has taken her place, or the little boy.

He stands up, goes to the window, looks out into the cold night.

Maria Sterzer,
aged 42, farmer's wife in Upper Tannöd

When my husband and Lois got back to our farm
they didn't need to tell me anything. I could see
something terrible must have happened from the
way they were walking, long before they arrived.
And when they were back sitting in our living-
room, both of them so pale, I knew it. You could
read it in their faces, the horror. For the first
few nights my husband kept waking up. The sight
of the dead wouldn't let him rest.

To think of such a thing happening right out
here. You can hardly imagine it. Not that I'm surprised to hear old Danner didn't die in his bed.

One shouldn't speak ill of the dead, so I don't
like to talk about those dead people. We live in
a small village here, you know. Any kind of
tittle-tattle gets passed on, so I'd rather not
say much.

All I will say is, I didn't like the folk at
that farm.

Loners, every one of them, and the old farmer in particular wasn't a good man. You couldn't get close to them, and I didn't want to either. I haven't even spoken to them since that business with Amelie.

Amelie was a very nice girl. She was a foreign worker on the Danner farm. That was still in the war. They made the POWs and all kinds of other people do forced labour on the farms. We had one from France here, our Pierre.

The men were all away in the war, except for Danner, he somehow fixed it not to get called up. He was thick as thieves with the Party people back then.

There were strict rules about the treatment of the foreign workers. But I didn't stick to them. Our Pierre worked on the farm, I could never have run the place all on my own with the small children and my mother-in-law, God rest her soul.

My husband was at the front, and later he was a POW, he didn't come back until '47. And thank God he did come back in the end!

Our Pierre liked working on the land. He came from a farm himself. But for him the place would have gone downhill fast, he worked away like the farm was his own. We all got on well. We didn't have much ourselves, but we shared what little we had with him.

When a man works as hard as that, you have to treat him decently. I mean, he's a human being, not a beast of burden. That's what I said to the mayor, I told him so to his face when he tried warning me off.

All he said was, 'You'd better watch your step, Frau Sterzer, many people have been strung up for less.'

I even got an anonymous letter. They were threatening to report me. All the same, I did what I thought right. I wasn't letting them get me down, not them.

Amelie was in a bad way. They didn't treat her well at Danner's farm. The old skinflint gave her hardly anything to eat, and she had to work like an ox.

And she was a delicate little thing. She didn't come of farming stock. She was from a city in Poland, I think it was Warsaw, but I don't know for certain.

I felt so sorry for her, poor creature. Our Pierre said Danner was chasing after her. Pestering and molesting poor Amelie, Pierre said, he even offered her violence. She showed Pierre the bruises, and she cried.

Seems that Danner once even beat her with a whip in the farmyard. Just because she wouldn't do as he wanted. She had bloody weals afterwards.

And do you think Frau Danner helped her? She didn't say a word. Far from it, she tormented and harassed poor Amelie herself the whole time.

I suppose if someone's been knocked about all their life they'll take the chance to knock someone else about if they get it.

Amelie couldn't bear it at the Danner farm any more. She couldn't run away, so she hanged herself. Poor girl. She hanged herself in the barn. In the very same barn where they found Danner himself and his family.

That's odd, when you come to think of it.

Old Danner hushed it all up afterwards, and the mayor helped him.

Pierre liked Amelie a lot. He sometimes gave her something to eat on the sly. There wasn't much we could spare, but maybe a piece of bread, some fruit and vegetables, and now and then a little bit of sausage. He smuggled it to her in secret. Once, when she was almost at the end of her tether, she told our Pierre about her brother. He was sure to come and look for her after the war was over, she said. And then she was going to tell him all about Danner. She'd tell him how badly they'd treated her on the farm, how the old man had been chasing her all the time, pestering her. Wanting her to do things she couldn't even mention to Pierre.

At the time I wasn't sure whether our Pierre had got all that right, because he didn't speak anything but French, and German after a fashion with me.

But I haven't been able to get Amelie's story out of my head, not since they found them all dead. In that very same barn. Who knows, maybe Amelie's brother did come to find her after all, and took revenge on Danner for her?

He wouldn't be the first. There are several who've taken revenge on their tormentors. You keep hearing such stories, off the record. There's plenty of skeletons in cupboards here-abouts. It was a bad time, and there were many bad people about then.

Franz-Xavier Meier,
aged 47, Mayor

It was around five when Hansl Hauer turned up at my house. The lad was quite beside himself.

'They've killed everyone up at the Danner farm,' he was shouting. 'Killed them all stone dead.' He kept on and on shouting it. 'They've killed every last one of them. They're all dead.'

And I was to call the police at once, which naturally I did immediately.

I drove to the Danner family's property in my car. I found Georg Hauer there, Hansl's father, and Johann Sterzer, along with Alois Huber, Sterzer's future son-in-law. He works for Sterzer on his farm.

After a short conversation with the three of them, I decided not to view the scene of the crime for myself.

A little later the officers from the local police arrived, and I considered that my presence was no longer necessary. I'm afraid there's nothing more I can say that might help to clear up this terrible crime.

Well, of course I was shocked, what do you think? But it's not for me to find out what happened, that's the business of the authorities responsible, in this case the police.

And that's just what I told the journalists from the newspaper, in almost the same words.

Oh, don't you start on about that woman too, that Polish foreign worker! I can't tell you anything about that. I am afraid the records of the incident were lost in '45. My predecessor as mayor could tell you more if he were still alive.

I was a prisoner in a French POW camp at the time myself.

When the Americans came here and liberated us in April '45, I wasn't home yet. They took over the then mayor's house and the village hall. They commandeered those buildings as their temporary quarters. The buildings were devastated by the time they moved out.

They acted like vandals. They shot at porcelain plates in the garden with their pistols. 'Tap shooting', that's what they called it. Just imagine. After they left, everything was laid waste or useless. Those fine gentlemen had taken what little was still of any use away with them.

So most of the files from the time before the fall of the regime had been destroyed too. We suffered severe damage, as I am sure you will understand.

And for that reason I can't tell you much about the events leading to the death of the Polish foreign worker.

As far as I know, the Polish worker, the one assigned to the Danner family, hanged herself. She was buried here in the village.

There were foreign workers everywhere. We prisoners of war in France were put to work ourselves.

Do you imagine we were always well treated? I for one didn't go and hang myself.

Nor do I see what this could have to do with the dreadful crime committed against the Danner family. This is simply an attempt to revive old stories. There are some people, you know, who just can't leave such stories alone. The war's been over for ten years. So let's lay those stories to rest once and for all. Times then were bad enough.

We all suffered. Everyone has his own burden to bear, but the world goes on turning. Times change. Wondering 'what if?' does no good. No good at all.

Of course there were injustices, of course there were moments of despair. Every one of us went through them. But the war's over. It's been over almost ten years now, time we started for-getting.

I was a prisoner of war myself, and believe you me, it wasn't easy. I was lucky, I managed to get home soon after the end of the war. Others didn't have as much luck, but what about it? What's over is over.

There are plenty of other problems, after all. But slowly we're going uphill in this country. Don't you read the paper?

I mean, look at the international situation. Right at this moment in time, since the end of the Korean War, the tension has relaxed slightly, yes, I agree. Our fears of another war are gone for the moment. But I can tell you, the commu-nists in Russia won't let it stop at that. You don't suppose this man Khrushchev is any better than his predecessor, do you?

Very well, so now the last prisoners of war are coming home. At last, after almost ten years, but that doesn't change anything, that doesn't change the potential danger from the East. That's why it was so important for us to sign the Paris treaties.

We have to act as an opposite pole. If only because — perhaps most of all because — the world has changed since the war.

That chapter, I would like to think, is now finally closed.

I do beg you not to go chasing after every rumour. I can guess where you heard that one.

And was that lady's own conduct always so far above reproach that she can point the finger at others? I wouldn't want to judge her, but one hears this and that.

I mean, there's her husband at the front, defending his homeland, and his own wife stabs him in the back, has a relationship with a Frenchman. He's fighting for the Fatherland and she fraternizes with the enemy.

The enemy is always the enemy, that's what we said at the time, and you can't deny the truth of it even now.

So kindly listen to me. The names of honest folk are being blackened, a whole village community is dragged into it. Just because a half-Jewish Polish worker hanged herself. The girl was probably unbalanced.

In my view drawing such conclusions so long after the event is more than distasteful. That kind of thing gets no one anywhere. So let's stick to the facts. Speculations of any kind are not constructive.

Particularly in the case of such an abominable crime. So if you would now excuse me...

O King of Glory,
O Son of God, Jesus Christ,
O Lamb of God that takest away the sins of the world,
grant them peace!
O Lamb of God that takest away the sins of the world,
grant them peace!
O Lamb of God that takest away the sins of the world,
grant them peace everlasting!

Anna Hierl,
aged 24, formerly maid at the Danner farm

I saw it coming. Was I surprised? No, not me.
Shaken, yes, I knew them all, I lived under the
same roof with them for a while. But surprised,
no, I wasn't surprised. Somehow I'd always been
expecting some such thing.

Old Danner liked to hire tramps to help with
the harvest, you know.

Why? Well, he paid them less. Simple. You can
pay a man less if he has a record and don't fancy
being reported to the police.

A fellow like that, there's times he's glad to
have a roof over his head and a hot meal. And
Danner was glad too, on account of he didn't have
to pay them much. That was old Danner for you.
Sly as a fox, and a skinflint.

I remember the old man showing one of those
good-for-nothing layabouts all over the farm. Now
that's something I can't understand. Gave him a
guided tour. Strutting about proud as a cockerel,

chest swelling, backbone straight like he'd swallowed a poker.

He'd take those vagabonds all round the house and the farmyard.

Showed them all the machinery, so no wonder if one of them happens to vanish a couple of days later, together with some of the household goods.

I always locked the door of my room when one of those gallows-birds was around on the farm.

There was one of them at the place once. Karl, that was his name, I think. Yes, I'm sure it was Karl. None of that lot liked giving a surname.

Easy to see why.

This Karl helped the old man get timber in from the woods.

It was right after the big storm in June last year.

They were getting in the trees that had keeled over in the storm. That's not easy work. It's been known for a man to be killed by a tree, or lose a leg. After a storm like that the trees are lying about all over the place. Sometimes stretched so taut, they spring right back when they're felled.

Well, after less than a week, off went Karl. Disappeared without trace, and a couple of chick-

128

ens along with him, not to mention some clothes and shoes.

And when someone tried breaking into the farm late last year I'd had enough. I looked around for a new job.

What happened then? I wasn't at the farm myself, it was Barbara, Danner's daughter, told me next day. I was visiting my auntie in Endlfeld, she was sick.

It was a Sunday, imagine that, a Sunday. While God-fearing folk are at church. I went to see my auntie straight after going to church. Barbara Spangler and her family, they went out into the graveyard after the service and then home.

When they got close to the front door, they saw that someone had tried forcing it. You could see the marks on the wood of the door, scratches everywhere. Like they were made by a chisel. It's a wonder the burglar didn't break the door right down.

Seems he'd been disturbed and ran for it. Just took to his heels and scarpered.

A thing like that didn't surprise me, I mean any of the layabouts that worked at the farm knew very well there was plenty to be had at Danner's place.

Not just chickens neither. He always had plenty

of cash stashed away in the house. That was an open secret. Anyone who ever worked at the farm knew it.

So well, like I said before, after that I didn't fancy staying on at the farm any more.

I was afraid the housebreaker might try it again, maybe at night next time. You hear about such things every day.

I mean, the farm's very isolated. Ever so lonely.

So I didn't want to be out there with them when winter came, not on your life. Twilight starts falling at three-thirty then, and by four o'clock it's dark. You can't see or hear a thing. So I packed up my belongings and went off. I found a new place right away.

If I hadn't left the farm then, who knows, I might well be dead now too. No thanks. I fancy living a little longer, I like life far too much.

Otherwise I could have got on all right with old Danner and his family. I know the rumours. He was odd, so folk say. Him and his whole family.

Maybe that's true, but I got on well enough with them. I did my work, and on my days off I went dancing or I visited my relations.

Work's work. You always have to work. No one's

going to pay you for idling about. A maid has to be able to work hard, and I like the work too. Then on my free days I make sure I go out and have a good time.

No, I was never pestered by old Danner. But I'd have known how to deal with that, believe you me. I don't let anyone take liberties with me.

What was the relationship like between Danner and his daughter Barbara Spangler?

Ah, I see what you're getting at.

Well, I can't really say, I didn't let it bother me, and anyway I wasn't at the farm all that long, just from spring to autumn.

Did Barbara Spangler sleep in the same bedroom as her father, like some people say? I can't swear to anything of that kind.

People talk a lot. I can only say what I saw. And it was only once I saw the two of them together, in the barn. I'm not even quite certain of that.

I went in and there was the two of them lying in the hay. Barbara jumped up just as I came into the barn. If she hadn't jumped up I wouldn't have seen her.

I acted like I hadn't noticed anything, and I didn't either. Nothing precise anyway.

None of my business, you see. Am I the priest or a judge? What's it got to do with me?

Barbara was ever so embarrassed by the whole thing, she said if she'd known I was going to go into the barn again she wouldn't have gone out.

Do I think those children are her father's? Well, what a question to ask!

You want me to be honest, yes, I do, but of course I can't know for sure. I mean, I wasn't there, was I? But I did hear Danner telling that layabout Karl how his daughter didn't need any husband. She had him, he said. I heard that with my own ears.

It was because that Karl asked about Barbara Spangler's husband. Where was he, he asked? Maybe he had his eye on Barbara. Well, he'd have got nowhere with her.

Neat and smart, Barbara looked, but she was a proud one too. Took after her father.

As for Barbara Spangler's mother, she never said much.

Grumpy, some called her. That's not right, though. Worn out by troubles, disappointed by life, that's what she was.

She just looked after her grandchildren and did the cooking. In the evening she always sat holding her prayer book. It was a very old prayer book, all shabby and worn. She always sat there holding that book and muttering to herself.

But once old Frau Danner did tell me her daughter's husband was a terrible scoundrel and had emigrated to America.

He got the money for it from old Danner. I still remember how surprised I was the old lady told me that, because she hardly ever said anything at all.

There she sat, and she started talking. At first I didn't even realize she was talking to me. She spoke so softly I thought, oh, she's praying, and she couldn't look you in the eye when she spoke to you.

Except with her grandchildren. She was a really loving grandma to those kids. I guess they were her only joy. Marianne and little Josef.

She can't have had a good life with that husband of hers, that's for sure.

He was a bit older than her, and I'm sure he just married her for the farm. It belonged to the old woman, you see, and Danner married into it. I think she was sometimes afraid of him, because otherwise a person can't keep her mouth shut all her life, can she? She must have been afraid of her husband, bad-tempered as he was. There was many a day when he didn't have a kind word for his wife. He snapped at her, and she always took it lying down. I never heard her raise her voice to him once, not once. Not even the time when he threw the food all over the floor just because he said her 'eternal praying' was getting on his nerves. He swept the dish off the table with his arm, and the food splashed all over the room. Old Frau Danner stood there and then cleared it all up without saying anything. Just stood there like a beaten dog. And Barbara watched as she mopped it up. Me, I wouldn't have put up with that.

And now I guess you want to hear the story about Hauer too, am I right? Yes, I thought I knew what you were after straight away.

Well, Hauer, he's their nearest neighbour. You can see his farm from the attic window. Yes, from the Danner farm they can look right across to Hauer's property. It lies on the other side of the meadows. A fine place it is.

Ten minutes on foot, I should say, if you walk fast. I never timed it.

Like I said, from the attic window you can see it, but only from there, that's the only place.

Hauer was chasing after Barbara. Very keen on her, he was. The little boy's supposed to be his. At least, he claimed to be the father.

Well, what I mean is he had himself entered as

Josef's father at the registry office, in the register of births.

Barbara Spangler's husband left right after their wedding, you see. Marianne wasn't born yet. That's what Hauer told me. Said he disappeared overnight. Here one day, gone the next.

Leastways, that's what Hauer said, but no one at the farm ever mentioned it.

Hauer's wife died three years back. She'd been very poorly for quite a long time. He told me so himself, and I heard it from people in the village too.

She had cancer, it seems, and she lingered on for a long time.

Just as soon as his wife was dead Hauer started his affair with Barbara Spangler. She was in love with him to start with, mad for him, she positively pressed herself on him soon after his wife died, he said.

Whether that's true I don't know. I don't get the impression that Hauer would be much of a ladies' man.

I'm only telling you what he told me himself. Hauer can get quite talkative when he's had a beer too many.

Barbara must have fallen pregnant right after they got together. Then, once the little boy was born — little Josef, that was — she suddenly didn't want anything to do with him any more. He just had to register that he was the father, and after that she gave him the brush-off, or least-ways that's what he told me. He wanted to report Barbara and her father, so as their relationship would be brought out into the light of day. Because it's a mortal sin, he said, it's against nature, and so on and so forth.

But then Hauer had had one too many when he told me the story. At the church dedication festival, it was. He told me all the ins and outs of it.

I wasn't really listening to the whole palaver, and I didn't understand most of it either, he was so sozzled.

I just happen to have seen for myself how once old Danner wouldn't let Hauer see his daughter, you could say he hid her from him. He said she wasn't at home. Although she was sitting in the little room next to the kitchen all the time.

If you want more details you'll have to talk to Hauer himself. I'm not saying any more about it, you just get involved in tittle-tattle that way.

Well, if there's no more questions you want to ask, I'll go back to my work now. Like I said, no one gets paid for idling around.

Evening has come. Everyone else in the house is already in bed.

His son Hansl, his sister-in-law Anna. She came here six years ago now, their Anna did. When the first signs of his wife's sickness were showing, and she wasn't able to keep the place going any more. Slowly, bit by bit, Anna took over the running of the household. She looked after Hansl as if he were her own son.

She nursed his wife when she was lying so sick up in the bedroom. His sister-in-law Anna unselfishly nursed her sister, his wife. Washed her in the morning, fed her. Cared for her all day long. Stood by her when it was clear what the end would be. When the sight of his wife's suffering had become unbearable for him, she moved into their bedroom with his wife instead of him. To be with her at night as well, ease her suffering, give her comfort.

By then he already found it impossible to be close to his wife. Her infirmity scared him away, he couldn't help her, couldn't be any support to her. As should have been his duty. 'For better for worse, in sickness and in health.'

He caught himself wishing her suffering would come to an end at long last. He was tired of the sight of her and her martyrdom. He could no longer bear the smell of sickness and death, a sweetish smell surrounding her like a cloak. He couldn't bear to look at her, so thin and emaciated.

He was out of the house as often as possible. Even on the day of her death he had been out all day. Had stayed out, walking around the place, even when his work was done. He'd wandered through the woods, spent a long time sitting on a rock. He would do anything rather than go back to his house. He didn't want to feel aware of the narrow confines of life and mortality.

When Anna told him the news he was relieved. He didn't mourn, he was glad. A millstone had been lifted from his neck. He could begin to live again. He felt free. Free as a bird.

No one would have understood.

Before the first month of mourning was over, when his relationship with Barbara began, he showed no shame or sense of guilt. After all, he was free. For the first and perhaps the only time in his life he felt free.

At first her interest in him surprised him. He doubted whether her feelings for him were genuine. But the readiness with which she gave herself to him laid the doubts in his mind to rest. Indeed, it made him long for her and her body even more.

Her body, free of the breath of death and infirmity. A body still enfolded in the smell of life, a body full of lust for life. Greedily, without inhibition, he gave way to that urge, to that passion.

Let the rest of the world consider his conduct improper and immoral – in Barbara he had found what had been denied him all his life before, not only in the last years of his marriage.

That marriage had always been more a marriage of convenience than the union of two kindred spirits. An arranged marriage, something usual among farming people. 'Love comes with the years. What matters is to keep the farm going.'

After a brief moment of fear when the desire he felt near Barbara frightened him, he indulged his sensuality without inhibitions.

When Barbara finally confessed her pregnancy to him he was happy. Only slowly did doubt grow in him.

Her attitude to him changed. She refused herself to him more and more often. Her passion for him gave way to increasingly open contempt. If he went to the farm to speak to her, she refused to see him.

But he couldn't retrace his steps now, he'd changed. Had given himself up to an addiction he had never known before, to a frenzy.

He knew the talk in the village. All the same, he had told everyone that the boy was his child, whether they wanted to hear it or not. His Josef. He had himself entered in the register of births as the father. And he *was* the child's father, he clung to that thought like a drowning man clinging to a rope thrown to him.

Josef was his son, and his little boy was dead. Murdered. He couldn't forget the sight of the child. He saw the dead boy before him all the time, whether his eyes were open or closed. The image wouldn't leave him night or day.

Anna Meier,
shopkeeper, aged 53

Oh, the misery out there, it's just terrible.

We've all been afraid here in the village since it happened. Everyone's afraid. Who could do a thing like that?

Who could simply go there and kill all those people in their own house? And the little children too, that's the worst of it. A man who could do that can only be out of his mind. Downright out of his wits. No one in his right mind could do such a thing. No, no one in his right mind.

The whole graveyard was full of people for the funeral. I never saw so many at a funeral before. They came from everywhere. There was a good many faces I didn't know at all, and I know everyone from around here because of my shop. I mean, they all come to buy from me. But there were people in the graveyard at the funeral that I never set eyes on, not in all my born days.

They weren't from around here. They'd come like

it was some kind of a show or a funfair. And they stared and gaped. Because it had all been in the paper, all that about the 'Murder Farm'.

'The Murder Farm', that's what it said in the paper. The man from the paper even came into my shop, wanting to ask me questions. He went round the whole village. And then he wrote that terrible story about the 'Murder Farm'. People even came out of town to join us in the graveyard. Terrible, it was. Plain terrible.

When did I last see Barbara Spangler? Wait a minute, it was just a week before her death I saw her. On the Friday. She came into the shop and bought a few things. I took the opportunity of asking whether they had a new maid yet, because I knew just the girl for them, a good hard-working young woman.

'Tell her she can start with us come St Joseph's Day,' Barbara told me.

So I told Traudl Krieger.

I blame myself bitterly, but how was I to know everyone at the farm would be murdered in the night?

These days it's not easy to find a reliable maid. It's not the way it was before the war.

All these young girls want to go to the big city

and work in the factories now. They don't want a place here in the village with a farmer. Well, they earn much more in the factories than on the land. And they don't get dirty either. It's not like the old days.

So Barbara bought her things and then she went out of the shop, and it was all the same as usual.

A burglary at the farm? Oh no, I really don't know anything about that. Once in autumn, yes, Barbara told me then someone had tried breaking into their farm. But that was some time ago. Nothing was stolen, folk said then.

But that's why Anna left. Anna was the maid they used to have at the farm. They managed without a maid through the winter. There's not so much to be done on a farm in winter. Now and then a casual labourer helped out about their place, Barbara told me that as well.

No, I never asked who he was. There were strangers at their farm quite often. Mostly they moved on again after a while.

You can be sure they weren't the sort that are registered with the authorities.

I liked Barbara myself, I don't know anything about the stories they tell. It's none of my business. I'd have my hands full if I made what folk tell me all day my business, wouldn't I?

I could write books, whole books. But it's nothing to do with me.

That story about Barbara and her father, there was a lot of talk about them, but nobody knows anything for certain.

I mean, nobody was there, right?

How did she get the little boy? Oh, you can imagine how tongues wagged here in the village. It made a great stir.

When it was known that Farmer Hauer was the father, there was a great to-do. Slut and tart, those were some of the nicer names they called Barbara.

I listen to the tittle-tattle and then I forget it again. In one ear, out the other.

I can remember that Vinzenz, Barbara's husband. He wasn't keen on farming. Not him. He didn't stick it out there at the farm for long. If you ask me, when it came to work on the land he had two left hands. He was in the wrong job farming with old Danner up at Tannöd.

You can say what you like about Danner, but he was a good hard worker. A proper farmer, he kept his place going well, even if he was an oddity.

I think he made sure he was rid of Vinzenz again. They say he paid him off, but there again that's just rumours.

What's a fact is that Vinzenz went off, here today, gone tomorrow. Some say he emigrated to America. But I don't believe that. He'll have gone back where he came from. He was from over the border, you see. A refugee. He came in '45, just after the war. They billeted him on old Danner at the farm.

But he hardly stayed a year. He wasn't the man to work on the land, not him.

It's terrible it all had to end like that. Terrible. I think about it all day. I can't get it out of my head. Who'd do a thing like that, I ask you? What kind of man? Not a man, no, it was an animal did it.

VICTIMS OF MURDER FARM AT TANNÖD BURIED
STILL NO CLUE TO MURDERERS AND MOTIVE

Einhausen. The members of the Danner family murdered in the isolated village of Tannöd, in the parish of Einhausen, were laid to rest on Monday with a large crowd present.

The murder raised painful questions, said Father Hans-Georg Meissner at the funeral ceremony, addressing a congregation of over 400.

'We are left behind in pain and grief. We stand by their open grave, unable to comprehend this heinous crime.'

As reported earlier, the body of farmer Hermann Danner was found last Tuesday, together with the corpses of his wife Theresia, his daughter Barbara Spangler, her children Marianne and Josef, and Maria Meiler, employed as a maid at the farm.

According to the findings of the post mortem, all the victims died as a result of massive trauma to the head area. The murderer or murderers probably used a pickaxe found at the scene of the crime as a weapon.

The nature of their injuries, say the police in

charge of the case, allow that assumption to be made. The investigating officers at the scene were shocked by the brutality with which the blows had been inflicted.

The bodies of Herr and Frau Danner, and of their daughter Barbara and granddaughter Marianne, were found by neighbours in the farmyard barn, hidden under a pile of straw.

The bodies of the other murder victims at the farm were found in the farmhouse.

The family lived a secluded life on their property. Maria Meiler had only just gone to work as a maid at the farm.

According to information from the police department responsible for the case, the above-named persons were presumably murdered on the night of 18–19 March. The findings of the post mortem confirmed that supposition.

There were also traces of injury to the neck of Barbara Spangler's dead body.

The possibility that this crime was a case of murder committed in the course of a robbery cannot be ruled out.

According to the neighbours, the family who lived so privately were prosperous. It is reported that there were large amounts of cash, jewellery and securities in the house.

The cupboards in the main bedroom of the house appeared to have been ransacked.

However, there is no clue to the identity of the murderer or murderers.

Maria Lichtl,
aged 63, priest's cook and housekeeper

If you ask me, the Devil took them. Yes, the Devil himself, Old Nick, he flew away with the entire family.

Father Meissner don't think so. He says I didn't ought to repeat such godless talk. But it's true, it's a fact, and it's our duty to tell the truth.

I've been cook-housekeeper for the priest here these thirty years. Thirty years I've been keeping house for the Reverend Fathers. I was cook-housekeeper for the old priest, Father Rauch. The Reverend Fathers have always been satisfied with me.

Oh, I've seen things, believe you me. And that's why I say that family out there was carried off by Lucifer. Even if the Reverend Father don't like to hear me say so.

Why, I saw him myself. The Destroyer, the Prince of Darkness.

It was when I was coming home from my sister's. She lives in Schaumau, and the way there passes Tannöd.

Yes, it was there, right there, I saw him. A-standing on the outskirts of the wood, he was, looking at the Danner farm in Tannöd. All black, with a hat on his head, a hat as had a feather in it. There's only one being looks like that, and it was him, it was the Devil. Only the Devil can look like that, I tell you, and when I turned to look again he'd vanished. The ground opened and just swallowed him up. Well, no wonder, is it? Not with the shocking goings-on out at that place.

You mark my words, when father and daughter get together everything's all topsy-turvy.

And the riff-raff he always had working on that farm! Not surprising if *he* comes, is it? Not surprising if Beelzebub comes to take them all away.

Rogues and vagabonds, a pack of ne'er-do-wells he had working on that farm. Shady riff-raff, the lot of them.

And his precious son-in-law made off too, disappeared overnight.

The Devil will have come for him first of all. Though they say that fine gentleman's in America.

What a joke! He'll have gone to join the Foreign Legion. That's where all the scoundrels go.

The old man paid him off. Everyone in the village says so, and then he went to join the French.

Oh yes, you can be sure that scoundrel went to join the Legion. Like all them scoundrels. If the Devil hasn't come for him yet then the Prince of Hell will be fetching him away soon.

That Barbara, she came to see Father Meissner with a letter.

With a letter from the French. No, I didn't see the letter.

But she wanted to speak to the Reverend Father, and then she left him a donation for the church by way of thanks.

I saw the envelope lying there, I saw it with my own eyes.

I daresay she wanted to buy absolution from her sins. Her guilty conscience was pricking her. Sitting on her like it was the Trud. But it was too late, the Evil One carried her off.

Oh, she was a proud piece, she was, and her father the same.

Never spoke to a soul as wasn't right in front

of their noses. It's a wonder the saints didn't turn their faces away in church of a Sunday.

That little boy of hers, he was her father's too. Everyone in the village knows that. But that fool Hauer got paid to say he was the child's father.

Still, you mustn't say that kind of thing, oh no, mustn't say it.

The Reverend Father likes to close his eyes and ears to such things.

That's how they are, the Reverend Fathers, always believing the best of people. While there's fornicating all around them, worse and worse all the time.

Old Danner has all the deadly sins on his conscience, every last one of them.

Chopping and changing right after the war, he was, and before it too.

He backed *them* a hundred per cent first, and then suddenly he's all for the Yanks.

He'd throw in his lot with anyone as brought him profit.

I wouldn't like to know what he had on his conscience. I could never sleep at night if I was to know it all.

And the police was after his son-in-law too. Folk say he was trafficking in something, and then he was gone. But for that he wouldn't have had to leave, not like that he wouldn't, not atwixt murk and dead of night, like we say hereabouts.

I've said it before and I'll say it again, the Devil took that family away.

There was a storm too, that Friday night.

Friday's a good day for the Black Folk, and the Trud, and the likes of them. Many a man has disappeared of a Friday, and that in a house where someone's already killed himself.

They wander around, poor souls, a-looking for their rights.

My mother told me such stories, and she had them from her mother before her. We have to listen to the old folk. By the Blessed Virgin Mary, may I fall down stone dead if it's not the truth I'm telling.

Reverend Father Meissner,
aged 63

I have been priest of this parish since the end
of the war. That's nearly ten years now.

But to the best of my knowledge such a thing
as this, a murder, has never happened here
before.

Many families in the parish are deeply dis-
tressed and shaken. Some won't leave their houses
now after nightfall. Community life has ceased to
exist. Everyone distrusts his neighbour. It's
nothing short of a tragedy.

We all believed the bad years were behind us at
last, life was gradually getting back on an even
keel. By now everyone who came from this village
is home again. Life had returned to normal — and
now this murder. Suddenly there's fear abroad
once more, people question everything. We see how
deceptive appearances can be in everyday life.
But let's not talk about that.

You want to ask me about the Danner family, I'm

sure. Ah yes, the Danner family. What the Danners were like. Well, I think old Frau Danner was a good Christian soul. A simple woman, but very devout. She often sought and found comfort in prayer. She was very reserved, and latterly her reserve was if anything more marked. I think she had already come to the end of her journey, and was preparing herself inwardly for life after death. As far as I can judge, she was loving to her grandchildren.

Her husband was a patriarch in all senses of the word, good and bad. What he said was law in the family. No one was to rebel against him, no one. No one was to go against his will. He was certainly a believer, if in his own way. I'd say he was a man of the Old Testament. Hard on himself, hard on his family.

His daughter Barbara. I thought for a long time she was suffering from her father's autocratic ways. But now I'm not so sure. Barbara had been greatly influenced by her father. I'd say the two of them were bound by a love—hate relationship.

On the one hand she admired her father. In her brusque way she was often very like him. On the other hand, I can't shake off a feeling that she detested him. Truly detested him.

She would never confide in me, although I tried

to induce her to do so several times. But there was the way she sometimes looked at him when she thought she was unobserved. To me, as a man of God, it was very strange. There was hatred in her eyes. Not love, no: hatred.

As a priest one is confronted with all aspects of human life. And you may believe me when I say I have seen and known much. It was recently in particular that I more and more often saw dislike, indeed venom, in her eyes.

The child Marianne was a dreamer, a little dreamer. I taught her Religious Instruction at school. She was very quiet and dreamy. A pretty little girl with blonde plaits. I cannot bear to think that she too fell victim to the murderer's hand. She and little Josef. Why, I ask myself, why can such a thing happen, why are two innocent children victims of such a wicked deed?

The mills of God grind slowly, but I do firmly believe that this deed cannot remain unatoned for. If no sentence is passed here and now on the murderer or murderers, then he or they will still not escape just retribution.

I am firmly of the opinion that none of us here can be the murderer. I wouldn't believe such a thing of any member of my congregation. No right-minded Christian can have committed such a diabolical crime.

What became of Barbara's husband? You mean Vinzenz?

There's a rumour that he emigrated to America. But the only certain fact is that he isn't here any more. He disappeared overnight. Vinzenz was one of those refugees uprooted from their homes who came to us in the weeks and months after the end of the war, in search of a new homeland, a new place where they could live and survive.

He found work on the Danner family's farm. It wasn't until Barbara was pregnant that she married Vinzenz.

I can't approve, of course, but directly after the collapse of the regime ideas of morality and order were in some confusion. After that terrible inferno, people were hungry not just for food but for physical closeness too.

It was one of the first wedding services I conducted in my new parish. Why did the marriage not last? Well, people may come together in turbulent times when in other circumstances they would never have done so. Many of these unions last, in spite of the problems of daily life, but others break under the stress of them.

Vinzenz Spangler was no farmer, and couldn't

get used to life on the farm. In particular he had a very difficult relationship with his father-in-law, and so he left.

Two years ago Barbara became pregnant again. Georg Hauer was entered in the baptismal register as little Josef's father. I wasn't going to condemn anyone.

The week before her terrible death, Barbara came to see me in the presbytery. She wanted to confess, she said. But then next moment she thought better of it. She seemed agitated, nervous. There was something on her mind. I told her to lighten her conscience.

At that her mood changed, she became defiant, almost aggressive. She had nothing to confess, she said. She didn't have to ask forgiveness for anything, she had done nothing wrong. Then she turned to go. I stopped her, because she had left an envelope lying there. I could have that for the church, she said, or for needy souls.

'Do as you like with it. It's all the same to me.'

And then she left the house quickly, without another word. There were 500 marks in the envelope. I still have them in my desk drawer.

There is perspiration on Barbara's forehead. In spite of the cold, in spite of the chilly wind blowing in her face, she is sweating. She hurries up the road to her property. *Her* property. Her father has made the farm over to her. She's her own mistress now. Her own mistress.

She has been to see the priest. She entered his room with some hesitation. She looked for an excuse. Wanted to speak to him, to ease herself and her conscience.

But then, when she was facing the priest, she stood there like a schoolgirl, couldn't get out the words she had been planning to say. He sat there behind his desk.

What brought her to him? Was there something weighing on her conscience?

And there was a smile on his lips. That omniscient, self-satisfied smile.

His request for her to lighten her conscience, and that smile too, the look in his eyes, had been enough to silence her completely.

Why should she do it?

Was this man to be her judge? Was he to sit in judgement on her life and what she had done? No, she didn't want to talk to him about it. Didn't want to receive absolution from any man. What absolution, why should she?

She had done nothing wrong. Wrong had been done to her. Wrong had been done to her since she was twelve years old.

For years she had fought against her feelings of guilt, had always done as she was told.

At school they were taught that Eve gave Adam the apple, and so both were guilty of original sin and were driven out of Paradise.

She hadn't driven anyone out of Paradise. She had been driven out of it herself.

To this day she sees her father before her. Her father, whom she had loved so much. She remembers feeling his hands on her body, those groping hands.

She had lain there perfectly rigid. Incapable of moving. Frozen. Hardly daring to breathe.

Eyes tight shut, she lay there in her bed. Not wanting to believe what was happening to her. Her father's breath on her face. His groans in her ears. The smell of his sweat. The pain that filled her body. She kept her eyes shut, tight shut. As long as she didn't see anything, nothing could be happening.

Only what I see can happen to me, she had told herself.

Next morning her father was the same as usual. For weeks nothing more happened. She had almost forgotten the incident. Had suppressed the memory of her father's smell, the smell of his sweat, his groans, his lust. It was all hidden behind a thick veil of mist.

She still wanted to be 'a good daughter'. Just that, a good daughter. She wanted to honour her father and her mother. As the priest always said they must in Religious Instruction. Everything her father did was right. He was the centre of her life, he was Lord God Almighty on the farm.

She had never seen anyone contradict him or oppose him. Her mother didn't. She herself couldn't either. With time, the intervals between the occasions when he came to her grew shorter. More and more often he wanted to spend all night in her bed.

Her mother seemed not to notice any of it. She kept quiet. Quiet as she had always been for as long as Barbara could remember. No one noticed anything.

In time Barbara got the impression that what her father did was right, and her disgust for him was wrong. After all, her father loved her, loved only her.

She wanted to be grateful, to be a good daughter.

Like the girls in the story of Lot and his daughters. Lot who had fled from the city of Sodom into the wilderness with his daughters. Lot lay with his daughters there, and they both bore him children.

That was what it said in the Bible. Why, Barbara asked herself, why should what was pleasing to God in Lot's case be wrong in hers? She was a good daughter.

She twice bore her father a child. She twice let herself be persuaded to name another man as its father.

The first of them, Vinzenz, came to their farm just after the war, a refugee from the East. He was glad to work on the farm and have a roof over his head.

It came easily to her to make eyes at him, and when she told him she was pregnant he was ready to marry her at once. He saw prospects of money and the farm ahead.

When her husband discovered the secret of her child's real father, even before Marianne was born, he threatened to see them all sent to prison. Her father gave him a considerable sum of money, saying that Vinzenz could go to the city with it, or even emigrate.

Vinzenz agreed to be bought off, and left the farm at the first opportunity.

Where is he now? She has no idea, and it was a matter of indifference to her at the time. The deal gave her a father for her child.

And life on the farm went on.

When she fell pregnant again, and this time there was no man around who could shoulder responsibility in the eyes of the public, her father had the idea of palming the child off on Hauer.

At the time Hauer had just lost his wife. It was easy for Barbara to seduce the man. The 'old fool', as she called him, swallowed her story with eager passion. Barbara had to laugh out loud. It was easy to pull the wool over a man's eyes.

Matters didn't become difficult until Hauer urged her to marry him. She must find out where Vinzenz was and sue for divorce, he said. Or even better, get him declared legally dead. These things could be done, he knew 'the right people', everything was possible for cash down.

She made more and more excuses, until she finally broke up with him.

The man gave her no peace. He stood outside her window for nights on end. Knocking, begging to be let in.

He even lay in wait for Barbara, urging her to come back to him.

Barbara was repelled by the man. Just as she had always been repelled by her father. The older she grew, the less she wanted to be a good daughter. Her abhorrence of her father and men in general grew greater all the time.

They were all the same in their greed, their nauseating lust.

With the years, she had learnt to make her father dependent on her. She loved it when he begged for a night with her, even went on his knees to her. She had him in her hands. The relationship had changed. Now she called the tune.

He must pay for his forbidden passion. Pay with the farm. He has made the farm over to her, on her conditions. She dictated the agreement to him. Now he depends on her and her favour.

Of course she wanted to buy forgiveness with her donation. She wanted to be free, and free also of a sin that she would never have committed of her own accord.

Time passes very slowly. The minutes and hours crawl by at a snail's pace.

Mick is still on the alert. The house isn't quiet yet.

He is waiting for his moment to come. In his mind, Mick goes over the plan once more. He's going to wait until the house is quiet and then go down into the barn.

The fire-raising trick. He's often done it before. It's easy.

The people who live in the farmhouse are lying in their beds. He starts a fire in the barn.

The cry of 'Fire! Fire!' would be enough to wake Danner and his family abruptly. Drowsy with sleep, they'd run to the barn to save what they could.

What with all the panic now breaking out, he'd have plenty of time to get into the house. The Danners would be busy getting their cattle out of the sheds to save them from the flames. In the ensuing chaos he'd find and purloin all the ready cash in the farmhouse. The Danners would be much too busy keeping the fire under control and raising the alarm to stop him.

Afterwards, no one would be able to say who first spotted the fire. His own tracks would go up in flames along with the barn, and he'd have disappeared into the woods by the time the blaze was out.

Mick leaves his hiding-place in the loft. The moment seems to have come. It has been quiet in the house for some time now. Carefully, he makes his way forward to the suspended ceiling of the barn. To the threshing floor there. He pauses. Hears his heartbeat, hears his own breathing.

A rustling beneath him. A thought flashes through his mind: there's someone down there in the barn! Why didn't he see him coming? How could he have made such a mistake? No point thinking about it now. Whoever's down there must leave before Mick can strike.

A second person comes into the barn. Mick hears a woman's voice. He knows that voice. It's Barbara's.

He doesn't recognize the man's voice. It's not Danner anyway, Mick is sure of that. What are they talking about? Mick can hear the voices, but he can't make out what they're saying.

He lies flat on the floor. Now he can peer through the floorboards.

The exchange of words is turning into a quarrel. The voices grow louder, the woman's rises, hysterical, shrill. The man takes Barbara by the throat, choking her. It all happens fast as lightning.

For a moment Mick turns his head aside. Tries to get a better view from another position.

When the two below are back in his field of vision at last, the man is raising a pickaxe above his head. Bringing it down on Barbara, who collapses without a sound. Lies on the barn floor. Her attacker goes on striking the defence-less body on the floor in mindless rage. Brings the pickaxe down again and again. It is some time before he leaves her alone.

Mick lies on the suspended ceiling of the barn, hardly dares to breathe, to move.

He's killed old Danner's daughter, the thought goes through his mind. Killed her like a mangy cat!

The unknown man bends over the battered body, lifts it. Tries to drag the lifeless form away from the door, further inside the barn. Away from the light, into the darkness.

Suddenly there are steps, a voice. Old Frau Danner is standing in the doorway. Mick holds his breath.

'Barbara, where are you? Are you in the barn?'

The old woman is struck down even before she has really entered the barn.

Mick turns over on his back, can't grasp the horror of it.

He'll kill me if he catches me, he'll kill me too, he thinks. Tears are running down his cheeks, he's frightened to death. He puts both hands over his face. Presses them firmly to his eyes. Tries to control his breathing, which is coming out of him in ragged gasps. Eyes closed, he lies there. But the madman down below doesn't hear him. Blind to everything in his frenzy, he strikes again and again.

How long Mick lies like that he doesn't know. One after another, they fall into the butcher's hands below him. First old Danner, then his granddaughter too. They all step out of the light and into the dark. Even before they can notice or even guess at the danger, they are struck down.

As they lie on the floor of the barn the murderer brings the pickaxe down again and again on his victims, frenzied, raging.

Lying on his back Mick doesn't have to watch the crime with his own eyes. He just hears it, hears the footsteps of the victims, hears them call for their family, hears the little girl call for her mother. Hears the pickaxe coming down, coming down again and again.

After an eternity there is silence. The silence of death.

It is another eternity before Mick notices the silence. He works his way slowly, almost soundlessly, over towards the steps down from the loft on his stomach.

The barn beneath him is empty. The murderer must have gone on through the cowshed and into the farmhouse.

Mick has just this one chance of getting away unseen and saving his own life. He takes a deep breath and climbs down the steps. Down the steps, out into the open air.

He runs breathlessly, runs on and on. His legs can hardly carry him. The cold night air burns his lungs. Every breath he takes burns them. He runs until he falls over and stays lying there on the bare ground. Gasping. The darkness has caught him. He doesn't know where he is. He has lost all sense of direction. He runs on from the house in wild panic. He wants to get further and further away from the house, the farm, the horror.

He sits there with his face turned to the window. His blank gaze staring into the distance. He sits there on his bed in his bedroom, sees things without perceiving them, looking inside himself, not out.

Behind him is his wife's bed. It has been covered with a linen bedspread since her death three years ago. He doesn't have to look at it, yet he sees it all the time. It stands in the room like a bier. Warning and reminding him. Day in, day out. He can even catch the smell of death. That smell still lingers on, drifting through the room like gossamer. His wife is ever-present in this room. Overpowering, like her slow sickness that seemed as if it would never end.

This afternoon's images appear before his mind's eye, his conversation with his sister-in-law Anna. She stands before him as clear and plain as she did two hours ago. She had come out to find him in the farm buildings. Said she wanted to speak to him, had to speak to him.

Incredulity and grief in her face.

They went round together to the bench behind the house. From there you can see the whole orchard in spring. You see the trees in full blossom. You see the land reborn. He loves that sight, he looks forward to it every year.

But the branches of the trees were still bare today, bare and dead from last winter. She sat down beside him. They sat there in silence. She was holding a piece of cloth in her hands. Only now did he see and recognize it. A cloth reddish brown with blood. The one he had used.

The cloth he had wiped his hands on. He had wanted to wipe away his guilt, wipe it away with the cloth, but it still clung to him. He had meant to throw the cloth away, but where? So against his better judgement, against all reason, he had kept it. Perhaps, the thought goes through his head, he didn't throw it away on purpose for her to find it, so that he could confess his guilt to another human being. He didn't want to be alone, alone with what he had done.

Anna put her arm around him and simply asked, 'Why?'

'Why?'

Why did he go out to the farm that night?

He couldn't tell her. He doesn't know why himself.

He wanted to talk to Barbara. Just talk to her. He didn't dare knock at her window. He had knocked at her window too often already, and she didn't open it to him, didn't speak to him. Yet he had been dependent on every word she spoke, every gesture she made.

Yes, he was dependent on her, enslaved by her. He had stolen around the house countless times by day and by night, just wanting to see her. He stood outside her window. He watched her undressing. So close and yet so far, beyond his reach.

The curtains open, she was standing there in the lighted room. So that he could see her and yet know she would never be his.

That evening he'd been drinking, Dutch courage. He didn't want to be sent away again. That's why he went to the barn. From the barn you could easily get into the house, he knew that, you went out of the barn along the feeding alley in the cowshed, over to the farmhouse.

She wasn't going to dismiss him yet again. Kick him aside like a stray dog. But the old man was the dog, the animal, it wasn't him.

He wanted to talk to Barbara, persuade her to come back to him. That was all he wanted. Just to talk.

And then, oh, the way Barbara stood there in front of him. Laughed at him, mocked him, told him to look at himself, look at himself in the mirror. She loved her father a thousand times more than she loved him, a stinking alcoholic sissy. She'd torn him off a strip, humiliated him. When he tried to take her in his arms she even hit him. He put out both hands to her throat. He took her firmly by the throat and pressed it. Pressed his hands tight.

He holds those hands in front of him now, looks at them,

hands covered with calluses from the hard work they've done all their life.

He goes on talking, he has to tell Anna the whole story. He has to confess. Not just the night of the murders, no, he has to get it all off his mind. It bursts out of him like a raging torrent, a tide sweeping him away with it. Anna is the branch to which he clings to save him. Save him from the torrent, save him from drowning. He wants to free himself from that compulsion. Free himself from everything that has been weighing him down for years. He needs her to absolve him.

'Barbara was a strong woman, she defended herself. Somehow she managed to get away from me.'

Why he suddenly had the pickaxe in his hands, where he got it from, he can't say, he doesn't remember when he first brought it down.

All he sees is Barbara lying on the floor in front of him. She wasn't moving any more, she didn't stir at all.

He tried to drag her away from the light, into the dark.

At that moment, there's old Frau Danner in the doorway. 'I didn't want her to start screaming.' Without even thinking, without hesitation, he struck her too.

One after another, he struck them down.

As if in a frenzy. A frenzy of blood-lust, his mind clouded, no longer master of himself. No, it wasn't he who struck them down, he didn't do it. The Wild Hunt took him over. The demon, the destroyer struck them down, all of them. He himself watched, watched as they were struck down. Couldn't believe he was capable of such a thing, couldn't believe any human being was capable of it.

He went on from the barn into the farmhouse. None of them must survive. Not one. He was going to kill them all.

It was like a compulsion, an inner voice that he obeyed. He was enslaved to that voice as he had been enslaved to Barbara. As immoderate in his desire to kill as he had been immoderate in his desire for her body. Yes, he had felt the same greed, found the same satisfaction.

He wasn't going to leave any of them alive, not one.

The new maid in her little room, he'd nearly missed her. Lord of life and death as he was that night, he almost let her live.

When the storm was over, he locked the barn and the house.

Only then did he take the key. The key that locked the front door of the house. He'd need it if he wanted to come back and obliterate his tracks.

His mind had suddenly become very clear. Clearer than it had been for a long time. He saw it all before him and knew what he must do.

He would come to feed and tend the animals. To remove all trace of himself.

He had freed himself from a demon, his own demon.

It must all look like a robbery. The more time passed, the better for him. He wouldn't be suspected. He hadn't done anything.

Except that he couldn't get little Josef out of his mind, the little boy lying in bed in his own blood. He couldn't forget that image.

Why did he kill them all?

'Why does anyone kill? Why does he kill what he loves? Anna, you can kill only those you love.

'Anna, do you know what goes on in people's minds? Do you know that? Can you look into their heads, into their hearts? I'd been locked up all my life, locked up.

'And suddenly a new world opened up to me, a new life. Do you know what that's like?

'I tell you, we're lonely all our lives. We're alone when we come into the world, we die alone. And in between I was caught in my body, caught in my longing.

'I tell you, there's no God in this world, only Hell. And Hell is here on earth in our heads, in our hearts.

'The demon's here in every one of us, and every one of us can let our demons out at any time.'

They sat there in silence.

After a while he stood up and went to his bedroom.

He has taken his old pistol out of the drawer in the bedside table. Now the gun lies cold and heavy in his hand.

Everything has fallen away from him. He just sits there, sits there calmly.

Christ hear us,
Christ, hear our prayer!
Lord have mercy,
Christ have mercy!
Lord, have mercy upon us,
Christ have mercy upon us!
Lord, hear my prayer
and let my cry come unto Thee!
Amen!